MURDER WITH MOTIVE

BLYTHE BAKER

~

When Sylvia Shipman's uncle plunges to his death on the eve of a catastrophic stock market crash, the verdict is suicide. But Sylvia doubts the official story after seeing a sinister stranger fleeing the scene. She doubts it even more after learning of her uncle's secret criminal connections.

With the help of her family's attractive new chauffeur, the mysteriously capable Miles, Sylvia chases the true killer through swanky jazz clubs and shadowed alleyways. But in her quest for answers, is she prepared to face an ultimate revelation more shocking than any she has imagined?

~

1

I never liked October.

I preferred the richness of the emerald grass of July, the sunlight streaking through the dense green leaves of the forests surrounding our summer home in the country. I preferred sitting out underneath the stars after spending the day by the lake in the heat, the kiss of the sun still fresh on my cheeks.

Yes, the ambers, golds, and rubies of the leaves in autumn might be lovely to look at, and the change in the air as Christmas drew closer gave everyone a bit wider of a smile. But winter meant dark grey skies and heavy snows. There seemed to be so little *life* left as the months dragged on.

The change in seasons did mean, however, that the number of balls and galas my family was to attend in the city would increase. It meant more jovial atmospheres, more times in which we had something to look forward to.

It was at one such gala that I found myself one evening, trying my best not to shiver in the velvet chair around one of the many circular tables in the room.

"It's a lovely place, really," Mother said, looking about, the drink in her hand sloshing against the side of the glass. "This hotel they've chosen...what's its name?"

"The Vandegrift Hotel," I told her, rubbing my hands over my arms. Why had I allowed the coat-checker to take my furs? I should have known it would be frigid.

Mother nodded approvingly, the blue peacock feathers of her bejeweled headband bouncing. "Yes, a fine place indeed. Brand new, too. We must be some of the first people to enjoy its splendor." She spread a hand out before her, chuckling to herself as she did so.

I heard a scoff from across the table, and my eyes fell upon Joan, or Jo as I had called her since I'd learned to speak. As she was only two years younger than I, we might have been able to pass as twins when we were younger, but not so much now. She and I both shared the same dark hair as our mother, but she had inherited Mother's pointed nose where I seemed to have a smaller version of our father's nose, slightly turned up at the end.

Jo's blue eyes, a few shades darker than mine, lit on

our mother now. "Mother, how many drinks have you had?" she asked.

"Only two, darling," Mother said, the color in her cheeks betraying her. "Don't fuss over me so. I am simply trying to enjoy this beautiful space."

It was beautiful, I would give her that much. I stared around, my arms folded tightly across my silver sequined dress that was far too thin for a night as bitter as tonight. The Vandegrift Hotel had been built just recently, and the rooms in which some of the guests were staying had never been graced with the company of overnight stays. This night would be their first, and from what I'd heard, they were as comfortable as they were luxurious.

The foyer where the gala was being held was more glamorous than many ballrooms I'd had the pleasure of being in. Windows stretched from floor to ceiling, draped in silk curtains of deepest blue, which seemed to blend seamlessly with the New York skyline that could be seen through the glass. The floor had been laid with polished marble tiles, alternating pearly white and ebony black. An elaborate staircase, nearly twelve feet wide, met the floor in the center of the room, like the neck of an elegant swan touching the surface of a pond with its beak. Above, the ceiling stretched all the way to the top of the building, each floor with an opening overlooking the foyer below. It almost made me dizzy, staring straight up to see the people mingling on the landings above, gazing down at me.

"Ah, I am pleased to hear you are enjoying yourself," came a voice from behind us. I looked over my shoulder to see one of our father's friends, Mr. Frank Morrow. He grinned at Mother, his honey brown eyes crinkling at the corners behind the lenses of his round glasses.

"Oh, Mr. Morrow," Mother crooned. "You *must* join us. Please."

"I cannot, Mildred, I simply cannot," he said, his gaze sweeping the crowd over our heads. "I must find your husband. It is...well, it's quite important."

Mother scoffed. "Oh, come now. Surely you aren't all still talking about that Wall Street nonsense, are you?"

His smile faltered slightly, and he only met her eye for the briefest of moments. "Well, yes, ma'am, a little. You see, it's – "

Mother waved a dismissive hand, some of the golden liquid in her glass splashing out onto her silk glove. She giggled. "Oops! Dear me. Now, see here, Mr. Morrow. I will not hear another word about it. All I have heard for days now is money this, money that." She shook her head, as if suppressing a shiver. "I understand you had a hand in the creation of this beautiful hotel? Let's discuss that instead. Something far more pleasant, yes?"

I swallowed hard. It seemed that, as much as she didn't want to admit it, she had felt the tension, too. I tried to smile at him, encouraging him as well. That really was a far more pleasant topic of conversation. I might have tried to steer him there myself, had she not.

Mr. Morrow seemed torn, his grip somewhat tense on the back of her chair. "That I did," he said with a halfhearted chuckle. "Connections are everything, as you well know. It seemed the perfect spot, and the perfect time..." His voice drifted off, his eyes passing over the guests once more.

"These lovely chandeliers," Mother went on, pointing at the six glittering light fixtures above our heads. "Are they real crystal?"

"They are indeed," he said, losing steam rather quickly. "No expense spared, of course." He let out a nervous laugh.

"I should think not, what with this marble flooring and crystal dishware," Mother said with another chortle.

"Have you managed to speak to Mrs. Nielson?" Mr. Morrow asked, changing the subject. "About hiring Phelps as your new butler? Or as a chauffeur?"

Mother shook her head. "Oh, he was dreadful," she said with a scornful frown. "An absolute bore, with that serious manner and complete lack of charm. Mr. Morrow, I shall have you know that I simply do not think we can ever find someone as good for our family as Theodore was."

"I am sorry to hear that," Mr. Morrow said, sending another nervous look around the room.

"She's turned them all away," Jo said, rolling her eyes. "Saying they are too dull. Too rigid."

"Well, they *are*," Mother said with a nod.

"Father wasn't terribly pleased, either," Jo said with a sniff. "He is getting antsy not having someone to tend to his needs, especially the driving."

"Jo…" I murmured. I then smiled up at Mr. Morrow. "I am certain we will find someone soon, we just need to have some patience, and perhaps more willingness to see that whoever we find will not be a perfect copy of Theodore, as attached to him as we were."

"True," Mr. Morrow said. "And especially in these times, having loyal help may prove to be worth more now than ever."

I tried to ignore the gnawing in my stomach as the conversation shifted once again, noticing the wrinkles in Mr. Morrow's forehead.

"The charity we are supporting this evening," I said quickly, hoping to quiet my humming heart. "It's for medical research, isn't it?"

He turned his gaze upon me and nodded. For a moment, it was as if he forgot where he was. "Indeed, it is," he said. "A fine cause, of course."

"Indeed," Jo said, arching a brow.

"Well, I really must be off," he said with an unnaturally forced smile. It was clear small talk was not something he was interested in. "If you see your father, please let him know that – oh, there he is now."

He hurried off, and my gaze followed after him as he wound his way through the tables spread all throughout the foyer of the grand new hotel. He had indeed seen my father, who stood in the corner furthest away from the dancing couples. I noticed the wrinkles in his forehead, even from this distance.

I pursed my lips, reaching up to spin the small silver key necklace that I wore between my thumb and forefinger.

"What's the matter?" Jo asked.

I glanced at her, not bothering to hide my concern. She would see through it, anyway. "It's Father," I said. "I know all this business with the finances has him worried."

"Oh, darling, do not worry your little head over it," Mother said beside me. She set her glass down so she might pick up another teacake, topped with candied cherries. "This has happened more than once, when you were all much, much younger."

"So you've said," I murmured.

"He does seem genuinely worried," Jo said. She waved her hand. "But I'm sure everything will be just fine. These things always seem to work themselves out, don't they?"

I didn't know if she was hoping to convince herself or us, but she turned her gaze away rather quickly to survey the rest of the room.

"Why hasn't that young man with the glasses come to ask you to dance yet, Joan?" Mother asked.

Jo rolled her eyes. "Oh, Mother, you cannot be serious," she said, folding her arms again. "I wouldn't dance with him if he were the only single man in this room."

"Really?" Mother guffawed. "My, I hadn't realized just how picky you have become. What's the matter with this one? Too skinny? Too tall?"

Jo clicked her tongue in annoyance. "*No*," she pressed. "He's a bit of a dunderhead, if I'm honest."

I smirked, despite myself. "That's not exactly kind, Jo."

"What?" she said. "He's perfectly all right, Mother, but he isn't for me. Perhaps some poor girl with barely a thought in her mind – "

Mother laughed at this. "Oh, my dear... I think I understand. What *you* need is to meet with my friend Eliza's boy. He's handsome, indeed. And smart as a whip, too, from what I have heard."

"Are you talking about Daniel Berkley?" I asked, brow furrowing. "Mother, he was married last summer."

"Oh...well, I suppose he was, wasn't he?" she asked, and laughed again.

"I'm going to go get some more coffee," Jo said, rising to her feet. "Why don't you accuse Sylvia of not having someone to dance with, too?"

"Oh, but dear, they shall bring it to you," Mother said. "Just wait for the waiter to come back around. It shouldn't be long."

Jo didn't answer, leaving us behind.

I sighed. It seemed it was time for me to go and make sure she was all right...or at the very least, give Mother some space. I didn't want to give her the chance to do as Joan had suggested. "I shall go after her," I said. "Make sure she doesn't get into any trouble."

"See that you do, darling, see that you do," Mother said, picking up her glass once again, bringing it straight to her lips.

I moved away from the table, following after Jo.

"Sylvia!"

I turned to see the bright face of Penelope Swanson, who smiled at me as easily as the day we met almost fifteen years ago. Gratefully, I slid into the empty chair beside her at the table and breathed a sigh of relief.

"Oh, dear. What's the matter?" the girl asked, leaning forward. She looked stunning in her dress of frost blue, with matching barrettes to keep her braid pinned around her head in a crown. "You look upset. What's happened?"

I forced a smile. "Oh, it's nothing much, really," I said. "Mother just seems to be overly...enthusiastic about this evening, and my sister is struggling to handle her exuberance."

Penelope smiled. "Your mother is quite a character," she said. "I see that a certain Mr. Lawson is not here this evening?"

I blushed and did my best to maintain the smile on my face. "Really? I didn't notice." How narrowly I had avoided discussing this...

Penelope's brows rose. "You can pretend all you like, but I know you well enough to know you are beyond relieved that he didn't show his face this evening." She shook her head. "Unbelievable. Good riddance, though, right?"

I tried to smile. "It really isn't as terrible as you are making it sound," I said. "He is a nice enough man but he and I are just not meant to – "

"A nice enough man?" she repeated. "Sylvia, he was caught sharing, from what I understand, a very passionate kiss – "

"I know what happened," I said. "He apologized and we agreed mutually that we were going to go our separate ways."

Penelope could only stare at me. "Your ability to say that with a straight face is astounding to me..." she said. "If I were you, I'd – "

"Well, thank goodness, someone I know!"

I looked up, smothering the pain that thoughts of Mr. Lawson drew up. "Oh, Jocelyn. How are you?"

Jocelyn Parker, no more than a year older than I, stood behind me with her hip cocked, surveying the room quickly before looking at me again. "Sylvia, I had hoped I would find you," she said. "Walter has disappeared again and left me all alone."

I pushed aside the strangeness of hearing my uncle's name used by someone my own age so casually, instead smiling at her. "Well, you are welcome to join us, of course," I said.

Penelope's expression said otherwise, but she hitched a somewhat believable smile onto her face as Jocelyn flopped down into the seat beside mine.

"What a *night*," Jocelyn said with a heavy exhale. "My word... Isn't this all so elegant?"

"It is indeed," I said. "Are you having a nice time?"

"I suppose," she said with a shrug, her bobbed, blonde hair bouncing. "Though Walter has not wanted to dance with me, not even once." Her bottom lip protruded. "I don't understand why. I only stepped on his foot twice the last time we danced."

I nodded, and opened my mouth to say something, but she beat me to it.

"He took me to that club, you know, on the east side? Oh, what was it called... I suppose it doesn't matter, does it? We danced all night long, out on the terrace, with the sounds of the saxophone our only company."

I nodded again, though my smile faltered. I didn't have the heart to tell her I had heard this story three times before.

"That was the night he proposed, you know," she said with a chuckle. She sighed happily, staring off into the distance with great affection in her gaze. "Oh, and did I tell you about the night that he bought me *this*?" She held up her hand to show off a glittering diamond on the middle finger, nestled beside her engagement ring, which was a hefty emerald, square cut and shimmering. "I had been gazing at it in the window of Burke's for...well, goodness knows how long. I must have walked by it a hundred times. He must have heard me talk about it, because wouldn't you know that just two weeks after he proposed, he gave me this?"

Penelope glanced sidelong at me, arching a brow. I understood. Jocelyn not only liked to talk but she also didn't care if everyone else remained silent.

"And this *bracelet*," she crooned, shaking her wrist in my face. "Have you ever seen such a beautiful bangle? But it pales in comparison to the dress he ordered for me. I asked for it, of course, but he was so terribly sweet as to pay for it." She laughed. "He might not have liked the price at the end of the day, but he told me that I was worth it."

I kept my smile in place, trying not to allow myself to grow weary as I often did when we spoke.

"Oh, but look who I am talking to," Jocelyn said, giving me a playful push on the arm. "You and your sister are *just* like me when it comes to pretty dresses, shoes, and hats. Fashion is just so exciting, isn't it?"

"Yes...very exciting," I said, though I couldn't quite put my whole heart into that statement. "I'm sorry, Jocelyn, but where did you say my uncle was?" I asked.

She gave a wave of her hand. "I hardly know," she said, bristling. "Likely still up in his room. He said your father wanted to speak with him about something, I imagine they are still there if he isn't down here with me."

I glanced over my shoulder, toward the corner where I had seen my father standing earlier, alongside some of his friends and colleagues. I could no longer see him. "Perhaps you are right," I said, my spirits sinking. "I'm surprise that your friend Madison didn't come with you tonight."

"She had a prior engagement," Jocelyn said with a heavy sigh. "No... I'm all alone, apart from Walter, and now he's off tending to business and whatnot."

"Well, given the current talk among the men in my family, I suppose they are all worried that this dip in the stock market is going to affect them," Penelope said, crossing her arms. "My father hasn't seemed too terribly concerned, but I know there are others who are considering pulling all their assets, out of fear of losing everything."

A small prickle of worry snaked through me again. "I am sure it will all work itself out," I said, repeating my sister's earlier words.

"Let's all hope that isn't too optimistic," Penelope said.

"Oh, I do hope they hurry it up," Jocelyn said, stretching her neck out, much like a peahen looking for her mate. "We have so many plans to straighten out for our honeymoon. Walter can't make up his mind if he wishes to travel to Italy, or perhaps out to California to see some of his relatives. *I* cannot understand what could possibly attract him out there but he seems to know what he is doing. I do wish I could convince him to move the wedding up, though."

"Why?" Penelope asked. "Aren't you to be married soon?"

"Before December, yes," she said, frowning. "But I think it would just be better for the both of us if we were married sooner."

*That is interesting...*I mused. *She seems genuinely worried.* "Well, perhaps after all this settles down about the financial markets, you shall be able to convince him," I said, giving her a smile.

"I certainly hope so," Jocelyn said with a shake of her head. "I simply cannot stand all this waiting."

That, at least, I could agree with her about.

"I am going to find him," she said, pushing her chair out, fidgeting with her silk gloves. "I will have him see reason, that leaving me alone at such a big party is just – well, it's just downright rude."

She strode away, determination in her steps.

"A bit of a handful, isn't she?" Penelope asked, her chin lying against the flat of her palm, her eyes following after Jocelyn.

"She's...unusual," I said with a stiff smile. "Quite different than my aunt was."

Penelope eyed me, pursing her lips, but said nothing more.

The orchestra's most recent song came to a close, followed by the applause of the dancers, their laughter piercing the somber mood at our table.

"I should be going too," I said, as if their joy and excitement had brought me back to my senses. "I told Mother I would look after Jo and see where she was off to."

"She probably just needed a break from your mother," Penelope said. "I shall be here, if you need me."

"You should go dance with William," I said, getting to my feet.

"Perhaps I should," she said. "Maybe it would cheer him up."

"And yourself," I said with a smile before turning away.

I started through the tables, trying to remember the path that Jo had taken. I couldn't see *her*, but her dress should be visible enough. She'd just had to have the same style of evening gown that her friends were wearing these days, in the same shade of apple red. Never one much for subtlety, that sister of mine.

I knew she couldn't have gone far, likely hoping to remain in sight of the young men congregated along the line of windows, apprehensively watching the young ladies as they passed by, hoping for a moment to ask them to dance. I steered clear of them for that very reason; I didn't feel in the mood for awkward conversation and bruised toes.

Surely, there had to be something here this evening to lift my spirits. Penelope had been a pleasant surprise, but she had her husband to keep her company. I'd hoped that Jo would stay with me, so I didn't have to face repetitive questions about the current state of affairs with Mr. Lawson...or lack thereof. Penelope, at least, had the tact to recognize his stupidity in all this, his thoughtless actions that had led to our parting of ways –

I breathed deeply through my nose. Mercifully, no one had come to ask me about him. Maybe they had the kindness to recognize I would not desire to speak of it. Maybe everyone was avoiding me for that very reason –

A terrible crash, followed immediately by a shriek,

suddenly cut through the pleasant hum of conversation all around.

I whirled in time to see the heads of every other person in the room swivel toward a table at the far side of the space, directly beneath the floors upon floors of balconies overhead.

Before people sprang to their feet all around me, I caught a glimpse of a man splayed out across one of the tables that was broken and splintered beneath him.

My mind went blank, my mouth going dry even as my heart knocked against my ribs, a bird caught in a cage, trying to take flight.

Instantly, the room erupted into chaos.

2

I had read in a dozen different novels about a pivotal moment in a character's life, one so earth-shaking that it changed the course of the heroine's very existence. One such book had described a terrifying moment as if time itself had slowed, every sense becoming heightened, every color vivid and sharp.

This had been but a fictional concept to me, and it had never troubled me that I might never experience the twisting, gnawing fear that had seemed so important to the stories I knew and loved. I had been quite happy to sit on my veranda in the baking sun, sipping lemonade whilst reading aloud to Jo, who napped in the hammock nearby.

It all became real, however, when my eyes fixed on the man that had fallen upon the table.

The first thought to cut through the confusion in my mind was that the scene didn't seem real. It *couldn't* be.

I had little time to look at the unsettling view, as many of the other guests quickly formed a wall between him and me, blocking the fallen man from my line of sight. These same guests, it seemed, also lost all sense of reason as they began to push and shove not only me, but to jostle one another out of the way so they might escape the frightening scene as quickly as they could.

I backed against one of the stone pillars that propped the ceiling up high above us. People swarmed past like schools of fish, moving as fast as they could. Shrieks, cries, and orders being barked pressed in on me from all sides, nearly overwhelming my senses. Disoriented, I didn't even know how to get to my Mother or Jo.

My breath coming in quick pants, I tried to peer over the heads of the crushing crowd, hoping to catch a glimpse of Mother's peacock feathered headband. It didn't help that, like Jo, she had acquired only the latest in fashion for the gala. Her distinction had disappeared, and I could not even begin to see where she might have been lost in the crowd.

"Get out of my way!" cried a rotund woman, shoving me off balance.

I gasped as I tumbled to the ground, slamming

against the marble floors I had admired just a short time ago. My hands came out in front of me, my arms buckling as I hit the tiles. I curled up in a ball as people stampeded by, and covered my head with my throbbing hands and burning, stinging fingers.

"He's dead!" I heard someone cry.

"He fell!" Another said.

Shuffling movement ceased around me, and I lifted my head enough to see the underside of a nearby table. I crawled over to it, using the seat of the chair to pull myself to my feet.

More people scurried by.

"Come on, my darling, don't look back – no, don't look!" said a man passing by, pushing the woman with him along. I heard no words from her, as she was likely too shocked to speak.

Angry shouts echoed over from the doors. Naturally, everyone was trying to get out of the lobby. Thunderous footsteps behind came from the staircase, people fleeing the floors above, either as news reached them or because they saw what had happened.

I thought of starting toward the door myself, beginning to feel dizzy. The room spun and I had to cling to the velvet chair in front of me until everything righted itself in my vision.

"Police! Someone must call the police!"

They were right, whoever it was. The police needed to be brought in, immediately. Still, I could see nothing of the sprawled man and nothing of the table. I was too far away by this point and had no desire to see him again. The image that I had seen, brief as it had been, would forever be seared into my memory.

I needed to get out of this room. My heart fluttered and my face grew hot. The room swam again, like oil paint dumped into a glass of water.

I looked around once more. The doors were entirely lost behind a sea of people. I would get lost in the crowd, if I wasn't trampled there first. I still had yet to find Jo or Mother, or Father. Maybe if I found some way around the hotel to the front, I could wait for them, find them.

A door along the side of the foyer, tucked between two of the windows, seemed entirely unused. Surely I could not be the only one to notice it, could I? Why was no one else using it?

I swallowed hard, time ticking by as I stood there indecisively. Was it worth being consumed by the crowd all trying to flee through the same door? Or was there wisdom in trying to slip around and meet my family out on the street?

The idea of getting caught in that stream of people again nauseated me, and so I hurried over to the side door. It was unassuming, painted black with no distinct markings upon it, and it opened without trouble when I twisted the knob. Biting, cold air rushed in, scraping like talons against my bare arms. I withdrew a few steps, wrapping my arms around myself, as if they could offer a little protection.

I would be cold one way or another, I realized, and hurried outside into the violet night.

I found myself on a narrow, stone landing in the midst of a lonely alleyway. Not even wide enough for a motorcar, the street boasted nothing more than a pair of wooden crates as tall as myself, a number of metal barrels, and some bits of trash strewn about along the edge of the building across the way. Just as I was beginning to realize that this exit must have been for the staff at the hotel, I turned to find the door closing behind me with a resounding *ker-clang.*

I pressed myself against it, trying the knob. It wouldn't give. I pounded my fist on the door. "Open up! Please!"

A screech of metal high above sent a shock through me. I threw myself against the door, looking up, frightened at the idea of something falling down on my head with no way to escape.

A dark shape moved swiftly back and forth on what I could only assume to be a fire escape, cloaked in ebony shadows as it was. Someone else had thought to use an alternate escape. As I watched, however, the man's movement, for the silhouette of a fitted suit became clearer as he raced down toward the ground, seemed frantic and erratic.

A knot formed in my stomach and alarms rang in my head.

"Sir!" I called out into the darkness. "Please, did you see what happened?"

The shape stopped for a moment before beginning his descent in earnest. He took hold of the last ladder, sliding down with both feet planted on either side of the rungs. As soon as his feet struck the stone road, he turned and fled.

My vision tunneled, yet my mind cleared in an instant as the bells continued to ring. "Sir!" I shouted, starting after him. Why would he be fleeing from me? Why was he all alone?

I raced to the corner of the alley, where I saw him veer down another intersecting alleyway to the left. I barely caught sight of the heel of his shoe before he disappeared around another corner at the end of another building.

He was getting away and there was nothing I could do.

"Stop him!" I cried, hoping that someone, *anyone,* could hear me.

"Is there a problem, Miss?"

A voice behind me caused me to leap into the air, emitting a shriek of surprise as I wheeled around.

I found myself face to face with a ragged looking man, with tattered clothes and matted hair. He stood before a metal barrel, dying embers glowing inside it.

His hands were outstretched over the barrel, his fingers exposed to the elements in fingerless gloves, as if to feel the warmth of the glowing ashes.

I took in his scruffy beard, torn hems, the patches on his sleeves... I wondered if he lived on the streets or was simply doing some sort of work out here.

Then I remembered what I was doing here myself.

"He – he is getting away!" I cried.

The stranger seemed to comprehend at once. "Which way?" he asked.

"To the left," I said. "He – "

Without another word, the stranger took off down the road, leaving only a rush of wind in his wake. He disappeared around the same corner that the escapee had fled down.

I stood there beside the barrel, the warmth of the embers lulling me toward them, a lullaby to my frigid frame. I didn't know what to do, whether I should go back to the hotel, or wait to see if the ragged man managed to catch up with the runner.

Better yet, I considered the polite manner that the stranger had used, how simple and plainly he had spoken to me. And...now that I thought of it...an accent? He was not from around here. British, perhaps?

I shifted closer to the metal drum. The shadows ensconced me, but my head darted around at every movement I saw out of the corner of my eye, shifted to gaze around at every sigh of air. This was not wise, standing out in the middle of a dark alley, an expensively dressed young woman entirely by herself. My jewelry alone would make me an appealing target.

I needed to go back to the hotel. This was foolishness. What had I been thinking, chasing after that man from the fire escape in the first place?

I had just turned and started toward the mouth of the alleyway when I heard that clear, deep voice once again.

"My apologies, Miss, but he managed to get away."

I stopped as if a spell had been cast upon me. He sounded ordinary. I hadn't known what to expect, really. I had never had the pleasure of speaking with someone from the streets like this.

"That's...all right," I said.

"Who was he?" the man asked, coming to stand beside me. His eyes stared past me before turning to look back over his shoulder. He seemed commanding, suddenly, like a soldier patrolling the alley.

"I don't know," I said. "He was fleeing a crime."

The man frowned, the expression only just visible behind his thick, scraggly beard. "A crime?" he asked. "Has something happened? Have you been attacked?" The way he asked the question gave me pause, and eased some of the tension that had risen within me.

"No, I'm fine," I said. "Someone fell, in the hotel. Over the banisters, I believe. He...he appeared to be dead, though I suppose I am not sure whether his fall was really a crime or an accident."

The stranger furrowed his brow beneath his wool hat. "And the man fleeing?" he asked.

"I don't know," I said. "I just found it suspicious that he was running away, in the opposite direction from everyone else."

"That does seem odd," he said. "Might I walk you back to the hotel, then? There are a number of street thieves in this area and I shouldn't like anything to happen to that pretty necklace or that flashy bracelet you're wearing."

I glanced self-consciously down at the items. "Yes, perhaps that would be wise…"

He nodded. "Come along."

I followed his lead as we walked away, back in the direction I had come from. I blamed my willingness to trust him so quickly on the numbness and shock preventing me from really feeling much of anything apart from the cold.

"My name is Miles, by the way," he said, a flash of white teeth appearing beneath the beard. "I am sorry I could not be of more help in catching that man."

"You do not need to apologize," I said. "And my name is Miss Shipman."

"Shipman," he said. "I believe I have heard the name once or twice."

It didn't surprise me; my father's name was well

known in the city, and we could hardly go anywhere without someone recognizing him.

"If you don't mind my asking, Miss Shipman, what exactly happened in the hotel? I thought I heard some sort of commotion, but you mention someone fell from the stories above?"

"That is what I believe happened, yes," I said. "I wasn't able to see much, not really. There was a great deal of yelling and rushing for the door."

"And yet, somehow you ended up out here," he said.

"I came out a side door and managed to just see the man hurrying down the fire escape," I said.

"And you think he might have had something to do with it all?" Miles asked.

"I don't know," I said, honestly. "His behavior just seemed...suspicious, given the timing of what unfolded."

"I can understand that," he said.

We reached the end of the alley, the bright street lights of New York welcoming me back to proper civilization.

"I have some connections that might very well help me locate this runaway of yours," Miles said, glancing up and down both sides of the street. A crowd had gathered out in front of the hotel and a pair of police cars were parked across the way. "If it's important to you, that is."

I didn't quite know if it was all that important to me, but then again, I felt compelled to bring this information forward if it might track down whoever could have had a hand in the unfortunate man's demise. "Perhaps it would be wise to simply take the information to the police," I said. "They'll be able to handle it."

Miles' face split into a broad smile and he let out a laugh. "The police?" he asked. "Oh, my dear lady, you have not had a great deal of experience with them, have you?"

I didn't know whether to smile or laugh along with him, and so I just stood there, uncertain what to say.

"Not that they're all incompetent, of course," Miles said. "It's just that there are a few of their number who aren't eager to listen to tips from people like me, or even from well meaning bystanders like you, if you understand what I mean."

"I believe I do," I said.

"Nevertheless, I will look into this matter for you," he said. "Find this man who fled the hotel in the midst of the chaos. It sounds a bit like someone who didn't want to be caught, which naturally makes me wish to catch him."

"And you believe you can?" I asked.

He nodded. "Oh, I am certain of it," he said.

"And what might you expect in return for such valuable information?" I asked.

He arched a brow, which disappeared beneath the

rim of his dark, wool hat. "Ah, so you understand the value of such things," he said, a half-moon smile brightening his eyes. They were an unusual shade of green, I noticed now that we were in a better lit area. "Yes, these sorts of things do not come for free, do they? Well, I shall not ask for much. If anyone you're connected with could offer me steady employment, I would be grateful. I am not a proud man and would be quite happy to take work in a restaurant kitchen or something similar. I need nothing special."

I blinked at him, my mind racing.

It struck me suddenly how much he reminded me of someone. Perhaps it was his accent but it was also in his charming demeanor, his pleasant mannerisms. He was *likeable,* and I had not even known him a quarter of an hour. He was willing to chase down a fleeing stranger if I wanted him to. That offered up a slew of questions but none so pertinent as that of how he seemed so capable. Why would a man with his readily seen characteristics be out here on the streets?

I glanced over my shoulder at the hotel, and a memory flashed through my mind. I thought of my mother's earlier conversation with Mr. Morrow. Our household, my father especially, was in need of a new chauffeur, and if that person could double as a butler, so much the better. This man seemed capable, friendly, charming...important characteristics of someone in charge of the day to day affairs of a household. He would likely be good with guests. He certainly smiled easily enough. His accent alone would be enough to convince Mother to bring him onto the staff.

"Miss?" Miles asked, peering into my face.

"My apologies, I was just considering your request..." I said.

It was crazy, I knew, but he needed work and we had a position to fill.

"Might you have some paper?" I asked. "I shall give you an address."

Miles patted the front of his tattered jacket, the top pockets, then the bottom. He reached into the front of his lapel and his green eyes brightened as he withdrew a torn piece of paper. He flattened the paper against the nearby stone step of the hotel, one of the stairs that I had raced down myself, and produced a pen. "Ready when you are," he said.

I quickly gave him our home address, which he wrote in a handsome, clear script. With each passing moment, and each bit of his character he unveiled, I felt more and more confident about my choice. He was an educated man. That much was clear. He checked the address with me before pocketing it. "And who shall I ask for on my arrival?" he asked.

"Miss Sylvia Shipman," I said. "If you would report there in the morning, I believe that would be the best time."

Curiosity glittered in his eyes, his head tilting slightly. "Your home? Are you quite sure?"

"We are in great need of a chauffeur who can also handle the duties of a butler," I told him. "Theodore, whose position you shall be taking, served our family for almost twenty years, and we are having difficulty finding a suitable replacement."

"I am sorry to hear that," he said.

"Yes, well... The position cannot remain unfilled, so perhaps my meeting you was a stroke of good fortune," I said. "For both of us, I hope."

"So it seems," Miles agreed.

He leaned to peer around me. "It looks like some of the guests are heading back into the hotel," he said, glancing back to me. "I shall search for this man, but you should go back indoors. It is growing late and I imagine your absence is causing concern."

I nodded. "Very well. Thank you, Mr. Miles."

"Just Miles is fine, Miss," he said, tipping his hat. "And I shall see you tomorrow, bright and early.

3

Miles had been right that the crowds outside the hotel had begun to thin. As I approached the front doors, it seemed that only half the guests remained out there. What became clear as I drew nearer, though, was the fear in the air. It hummed, shrouding the whole street. I passed by a woman clutched tightly in her husband's arms, crying hysterically. Not far from them stood a pair of men arguing.

"You said you went down the hall," said the shorter of the two. "To go back to your room. And you didn't see anything?"

"How could I have seen anything?" asked the other, the scrawnier of the pair. "How could I have known I should be looking for someone to throw themselves over the banister? Are you suggesting this is somehow *my* fault?"

I hurried past them, squeezing between another few groups, their worried whispers pricking my ears like the buzz of angered bees.

I looked around for my family but could not seem to find any of them.

I did, however, find Penelope and her husband, William.

"Oh, Sylvia..." she said, throwing her arms around me as soon as I approached her. "Thank heavens you are all right."

"Of course I am," I said. "Why wouldn't I be? It was a man who fell."

Penelope pulled away, her eyes suddenly as hard as the marble tile floors. "You...didn't hear?" she asked.

My stomach dropped. "No. What is it?" I asked.

She looked up at her husband, who gave me a sympathetic frown, his lips pinching tightly together.

Thoughts raced through my head, terrible thoughts. Was he not the only one? Were other people dead? Was it someone I knew?

"Sylvia..." Penelope said, in a tone so gentle my skin crawled as I realized exactly what a terrible truth she was about to speak. "...People are saying it's your Uncle Walter."

Stunned, I could only stare at her as her words pierced

the thick fog that flooded my mind. My...uncle? Out of the hundreds of people that had been there that night, somehow it happened to be someone in my own family?

"It – it can't be," I said, the words spilling out before I could stop them. "Have they checked for certain? It couldn't have been him. He was upstairs with my father. There would have been people with him. We should find my father, he will find Uncle Walter for us – "

I started away but I stopped short as Penelope grabbed hold of my wrist.

My mouth went dry and I wished I could shut my ears. I didn't want to hear it.

"I just spoke with him, not even an hour ago," I said. My uncle's face appeared in my mind, smiling as he always did, his features so similar to my father's. He had arrived late to the gala but made it a point to stop and talk to Jo and me. We talked of the weather and the chill in the air. Inane, useless things.

The image of him smiling as he turned away from us, as he went to find my father, slowed to a snail's pace. If he had stayed and talked to us a little longer, would it have changed his fate? Would whatever accident that had occurred have been waylaid?

Uncle, please don't go, I heard my own voice calling out to him in the memory, as if a strong enough will could shift the reality around me, as if I could change the past.

I rounded on Penelope. "What happened?" I asked. "Where is my family?"

"They were brought back indoors," Penelope said. "To identify him. Though not without the needlessly nosy guests who decided to follow them in."

My eyes shifted to the large, glass front doors of the hotel. They had once seemed so inviting, so glamorous. Now, hatred poured from my heart like a seeping wound. A black mar stained the place, one that I knew could not be blotted out.

Whirling around, I looked for Miles, wondering wildly if he had followed after me for some reason.

"Who are you looking for?" Penelope asked.

"No one," I lied, far too easily and far too quickly.

I looked at the doors again. I knew what I had to do but it was the very last thing I *wanted* to do.

"Shall we come with you, Sylvia?" Penelope asked.

I shook my head. I would have to face my parents and their grief sooner or later, I knew. I could not run from it forever. I took one step and then another toward the doors. I wondered if someone had put lead weights in my shoes, as heavy as they felt. I became aware of each breath, as well, moving in and out of my lungs. Breath of life. Breath that my uncle no longer breathed.

I stepped inside, and the change in atmosphere turned my stomach. The pressed tablecloths and gleaming dishware that had seemed so warm and inviting upon my first arrival now seemed lifeless, hollow, and representative of a time long past. Their beauty mocked me, blatantly reminding me that I was not to partake in the pleasure of their company and use for some time to come.

I heard my mother before I saw her. Even amidst the large crowd that had gathered back inside the room, surrounding the scene of my uncle's demise as if it were a sporting event, I could pick out her wailing sobs.

I started toward her like a prisoner approaching the gallows and no one said anything to me as I was enveloped by the little group. They stood off to the side of the rest of the crowd. I caught a glimpse of a rope tied between some of the chairs, blocking the guests from getting any closer to the broken table.

Mother didn't seem to notice me. Jo gave me a brief, petrified look. Father stood off to the side with a pair of men. It wasn't until I looked straight at them that I realized they were police officers.

At once, I heard Miles' voice in my mind, assuring me that not *all* of the police were incompetent. It made me all the more nervous. What if these officers were inexperienced? What if they couldn't figure out what had happened?

Their presence explained the rope tied between the chairs. With the body of a man who had died in such a public place, it was only natural that they wished to preserve the scene untouched by the crowds, while they investigated. They must have been called as soon as it all happened.

My throat went tight as I thought about Uncle Walter falling from such a height –

"Where have you been?" Jo asked under her breath.

"Outside, looking for you," I murmured in return. "What happened?"

Jo shrugged. "I hardly know anything."

I could scarcely blame her for her clipped answer. I could barely strangle out a follow up question.

"But it is...it was – " I managed to get out.

She nodded her head, her face looking greenish.

It wasn't as if I had any hope otherwise but to have it confirmed by her, knowing she would have no reason to lie, was difficult.

"Excuse me, pardon me!" came a voice over the crowd. "I must ask you all to leave the hotel."

Murmured protests arose from the crowd, but the officer, who I spotted standing on top of one of the tables, his footprints ruining the stark white tablecloth, waved his hands above his head. "This is a crime scene. If you have any information about this man's death, please find one of the officers scattered around the room. But for those of you who are only here to gawk – "

"What about those of us who are guests of the

hotel?" called a man through the crowd. "We paid good money to stay here!"

More agreements rose from the crowd.

"You will have to speak with the management about being reimbursed for your stays," the officer said. "We cannot have anyone staying here until we have learned exactly what occurred. Once everything has been cleared, you will be able to return, perhaps even as early as the day after tomorrow."

Angry protests came from the guests. I could only stand there, dismayed. How could these people care so little for a life that had ended in their presence not even an hour ago?

The officers began to usher guests toward the doors, but they left us where we were. Some of them came over to move us away, but when the pair Father had been standing with told them we were family of the victim, we were allowed to linger.

When the room had been cleared, I could finally see the scene.

The table remained where it had always been, caved inward on itself, its tablecloth askew, its splintered legs stretched up toward the ceiling.

Uncle Walter, mercifully, no longer lay there. For a fleeting moment, I imagined that he had somehow awoken, gotten up and walked away. If only he had.

"If you wish to identify him now, the deceased has been laid behind the stairs so as not to be seen by the crowd," said a tall man with a thick, dark beard and matching moustache. He wore the same uniform as the rest of the officers but the air of authority about him told me he must be of higher rank, directing orders as he did. "If you would prefer, you could wait until he has been moved to the morgue, but as you are already here..."

"Soonest is best," my father interrupted in a hollow sounding voice. "I wish to know at once."

The officer nodded. "I am sorry for your loss."

Such words didn't feel like enough. No words would, I realized with a sinking in my stomach.

Jo reached for my hand, which I allowed even though my palms had grown clammy. She squeezed tightly, so that the bones within my fingers ached as they rubbed together like a bundle of sticks.

Mother hung back, eyeing the staircase, as if expecting it to jump to life right in front of her. Father, however, made his way around to where the officer led him.

I swallowed hard, not certain where my eyes should fall.

Neither Jo nor I wanted to take the first step forward. "Do we have to?" she muttered beneath her breath.

"No, I suppose we do not all have to see him," I said quietly, and so we waited.

Father returned a moment later, most of the color

drained from his face. He pursed his lips and did not look up at us as he walked by.

"It's him, all right," he said, in a far steadier tone than his face had suggested. "No doubt about it."

"What should we do?" Mother asked. It was not often that I heard such fear in her voice, rendering it so strange to my ear that I might not have immediately recognized it to be her, had I not known she stood so close.

"Have the coroner's office take him," Father said, clasping his hands behind him, surveying the room. "See what they can make out."

"Do they know what happened?" I asked, taking a step toward him and away from the stairs. Chills passed down my spine at the very idea of Uncle Walter's body being so close and so lifeless. "Do they know why he fell?"

Father turned his grey eyes upon me and I saw... nothing. No sorrow, no fear, no anger. Only empty pupils without any discernible emotion. "No," he said, and it was of little surprise that his answer held no feeling. He might as well have been speaking to the wall. "And frankly, that matters very little."

"What do you mean?" Jo asked. "Was it an accident?"

Surely it could only have been an accident... "What else could it have been?" I asked.

Jo turned to me. "You've read enough novels, haven't you? Heard enough stories?"

"Are you saying someone could have done this to him?" I asked. Despite the doubt in my voice, her suggestion had been my own first instinct as well. Hadn't it been the reason for my pursuit of the man from the fire escape?

"Or he did it to himself," Jo said, glancing warily over her shoulder. "Just like that man at the bank three years ago – "

"Enough," Father said, glaring at the two of us. "There will be no more talk of this."

"But Father," I said. "What if – "

"No," he said, firmly. "I will not hear of this. I will not tolerate it."

"Your father is right," Mother said, trying to gather herself as she straightened the feathery headband on her head. "It's over and done with. I suppose it – it doesn't matter how it happened."

I could only stare at her.

"Now, come along," she said, turning away, the hem of her glittering evening gown swooshing around her ankles. "Let's go home."

I did not particularly wish to argue over the subject but it unsettled me how deliberately silent the pair of them were being as we made our way back home, almost as if by unspoken agreement. How could they wish to remain ignorant of the cause of my uncle's death?

IT SHOULD HAVE BEEN a great relief to arrive at Sutton Place, to our home that was not yet three years built, but the knots in my stomach still would not loosen. Try as I might, I could not get my mother to speak to me. She waved me away every time I tried to discuss what happened, and shook her head like a child. I half expected her to put her fingers petulantly in her ears as we strode up the front steps of our rowhouse, where the front door was painted in the same fashionable bright blue as our neighbors.

"Is this our responsibility now?" I asked, turning my attention to my father as Mother hurried down the hall, the housekeeper following swiftly after her with a fan and a steaming cup of coffee in hand. "Are we meant to – to deal with all the matters concerning his death?"

"What do you mean?" Father asked, passing his hat and jacket to one of the servants, whose turn it was to serve as the fill-in butler for the day. "No. No, I'm certain Jack will take care of it."

I frowned as he strode toward the staircase that ran up the right side of the main hall. Uncle Jack was the eldest brother, certainly, but he lived some distance up the Hudson River, nearly an hour's drive from here. He rarely deemed it worthwhile to take note of our affairs. "Hasn't it been nearly two years since you spoke to him?"

"I'll have you know that he sent me a letter just six weeks ago," Father said over his shoulder. "I'll ring him up and tell him he'll have to use some of that inheritance money to bury Walter. I certainly am not covering those expenses."

I stood at the foot of the stairs, my knees aching from worry, my stomach twisting and small. I didn't know if I would be able to eat for the next three days... or even be able to *look* at food. "How can you be so callous about all this?" I asked.

He stopped at the top of the stairs and glanced down at me. "I cannot spend time thinking this over when there is – there is so much else to be getting on with."

"You are telling me you're more concerned about predictions of economic disaster, than your own brother's death?" I asked.

His brow furrowed. "This is not like you, Sylvia." He stared at me, long and hard, just like he would until I quieted as a child. "We are done discussing this. Have I made myself clear?"

All the questions, all the concerns, backed up in my throat, sticking there as if I'd swallowed a bag of marbles.

He seemed to take my silence for agreement. "Good," he said. "I will be in my study. I have...a great deal that needs to be dealt with. Especially now."

I listened to his footsteps fade on the carpeted hallway above my head, followed predictably by the *ker-thunk* of his door closing behind him.

I looked about, and found Jo standing nearby, leaning against the wall as she stared up the staircase. "I don't understand it, either."

I turned to her. "Am I losing my mind? Why does it seem as if I am the only one who is concerned about what happened?"

"Because you are," Jo said. "Father is too preoccupied and Mother just...she simply *won't* deal with it. I don't think she could. If she did, she would fall to pieces."

*Perhaps that would be the better of the two possibilities...*I thought. "Then what are you and I to do?"

"Nothing," Jo said, pushing away from the wall. "It isn't our responsibility either."

"How can you be so calm?" I asked.

Jo threw me a grin over her shoulder, but it seemed fragmented, like a reflection in a broken mirror. "I'll take that as a compliment, dear sister. It seems that my acting *has* improved."

With that, she swept off up the stairs after father, presumably on the way to her quarters.

Alone and terribly aware of the silence pressing in

around me, I made my way to the back of the house and out into the back garden overlooking the East River.

The cold midnight wind rushed against me. Instead of wincing, I drew it in deeply. Despite the heady, fishy scent that being downwind of the river occasionally brought, it at least cleared my mind at the same time it calmed my nerves.

The city stretched up and down the edge of the river. Lights glittered in the buildings across the water, their reflections dancing as the water rushed past. I gazed out at the bridge that spanned the river off to my left, a magnificent suspension bridge that never failed to ground me in my surroundings. I might not have grown up in this house, but we had previously lived just a few miles north, and so this scene had always been in my sightline. A constant, consistent presence...

I wrapped my arms around myself, talking slow steps toward the river. A fog horn echoed somewhere downstream.

How could it be that another presence in my life, one almost as constant and consistent as the bridge in the distance, was now gone? I had seen Uncle Walter just this evening. Spoken with him. Everything had seemed so ordinary.

Jo had always called me our uncle's favorite, and that was a tall order, given I was one of so many nieces and nephews. Every time I saw him, we would discuss our favorite shared interest; the violin. I never talked of it with anyone but him, but he was part of the reason I began to play in the first place.

My eyes stung and I pinched them shut.

And now...he was gone.

How?

Why?

I sank down onto the painted, wrought iron bench. The icy metal seeped through the skirts of my dress and the cold snaked over my flesh. I didn't care, as it reminded me that at least I was feeling *something*, unlike either of my parents.

Maybe they don't know what to feel, I thought to myself, staring out at the waves of the river lapping up against the bank, the lights shimmering against the surface of the water as dark as ink. *Maybe they are simply numb to it all.*

That might be worse. It could mean their breakdowns would happen later, after Joan and I had worked through it. It was difficult to imagine what Father must eventually feel, as Uncle Walter was his brother. I had trouble believing he could permanently ignore the death in favor of his own financial worries and the concerns of Wall Street. He might be surprisingly calm on the surface but I had seen that he was shaken at the sight of his deceased brother lying behind the staircase, back at the hotel.

It struck me that something about this whole affair

did not quite make sense. There was a piece that didn't fit. What about the man I had seen fleeing down the fire escape?

A horn honked somewhere behind me, and I yelped, leaping to my feet.

Panting, my ragged breath filling the cold air around me like morning fog, I whirled around.

*Just a car...*I told myself. *Nothing more.*

I hurried inside after that, not wanting to give anything else in the wide, vast city a reason to quicken my heart. I didn't know how much more stress I could handle.

I slipped through the back door, closing off the life of the city behind me. It could stay there. It cared little for my problems and it only grieved me further to realize that. People everywhere were existing right alongside me, passing through the same moment in time, but likely with many different points in life; babies were being born, proposals made, toasts shared, arguments trudged through...and even death.

I stopped when I heard the sound of an unfamiliar male voice in the next room. Who could possibly be visiting at a time like this?

I pushed open the door to the parlor and found my mother sitting alone before the radio, in her usual chair near the fireplace. The male voice continued speaking over the radio, and Mother slapped her knee, a drink in her other hand sloshing out onto her lap as she gave an unnaturally high-pitched laugh.

"Mother?" I asked, troubled but not especially surprised to find her in this state at such a time. "What are you listening to?"

"Oh, Sylvia, dear. You should hear this," she said, pointing to the radio. I heard laughter on the track, followed by the dry, deep voice of the man again. "He's a *riot*, I tell you. A riot!"

For better or worse, it seemed Mother had found a means of coping.

"Mother, please shut it off," I said. "I realize you want to distract yourself but hiding from our loss will not help."

She shook her head. "Darling, you mustn't allow yourself to be so consumed by this," she said. "Your uncle would not have wanted any of us to make ourselves ill with grief. It's over and done with, just as your father said."

"But Mother...he was Father's brother – " I said.

"I know perfectly well who he was," she said sharply, her eyes glazing. "I haven't – I am perfectly fine. I know who he was."

"Does it not trouble you?" I asked.

"It is one of the burdens of being so wealthy," she snapped. "People want our money and will go to great lengths to get it."

"What do you mean?" I asked. The man rushing

away in the darkness swept through my mind again. "Do you think someone killed Uncle Walter?"

She shrugged, her drink swirling around the lip of the glass again. "Who can know? All I know is this isn't the first time we've lost relatives because of money... and it certainly will not be the last."

*A burden of being so wealthy...not the first time we've lost relatives because of money...*I mused.

There was the truth at last, it seemed. The dark, underlying truth about wealth. In a world where people killed for money, possessing it could make one a target. Was that what had happened? Had Uncle Walter been targeted? "It's horrible to think someone could have – "

"What did I say?" Mother snapped. "Do not worry yourself over it."

How could I not?

"I must go to bed," Mother said abruptly, getting to her feet and turning off the radio. "Good night, Sylvia."

I watched her go, unable to echo her departing words.

There was absolutely nothing *good* about this night. Nothing at all.

4

CRASH.

I sat straight up, my heart pounding in my chest before I even fully realized where I was or what time it was. My eyes itched, every muscle in my arms and legs ached, and my head swam as if I'd been drinking too much champagne. I rubbed my face, turning to see sunlight peeking through the seams of the thick curtains.

Pounding echoed from somewhere downstairs, and it took me a few moments to realize it was not just the noise of my own heartbeat in my ears.

What was that? I wondered, slipping out from beneath my blankets.

Cold struck me like a gale and I shivered as I reached for my dressing gown. Pulling it over my sleeves, I started as frantic footsteps raced down the hall.

I rushed to the door, peering out just in time to see a trio of servants hurrying toward the staircase.

Another *crash* emanated from somewhere below.

I gripped the doorframe. What in the world was happening?

"No, the *other* crate!" my father roared from his study on the floor beneath me. "Must I walk you through everything?"

Another muffled voice answered, before my father's holler came in reply.

"Then *make* them buy! Do whatever you can to change their mind! I cannot lose that investment!"

Money, it seemed, and its concerns, were what had begun the day.

Distant car horns blared out in the street, one right after the other. Insistent, frequent.

Goosebumps formed on my skin. Something didn't feel quite right.

I crossed back through my room to the window, pulling back the shades. My jaw fell open when I saw the cars backed up along our street and people hurrying this way and that along the sidewalks. It might as well have been the rush before Christmas, when everyone hurried about to finish their shopping and gift wrapping and visiting with family. There was something much, much different in the air, however. Something dreadful.

I hurried to dress, pulling on a navy blue skirt with double rows of gold buttons down the front and a simple matching blouse. The mournful combination suited my mood, as well as the tense atmosphere I sensed around me.

All the while I did up my buttons, I continued to hear more banging and slamming from downstairs. The shouts and barked orders might not have been clear but the emotion behind them certainly was.

Whatever had happened in the middle of the night had turned the house upside down.

*Surely this has to be something to do with Uncle Walter...*I thought as I ran my fingers through my bobbed hair, trying to smooth down the dark locks quickly. I didn't wish to spend the time properly combing it, nor did I have the strength to look my reflection in the eye. It didn't matter how long I had tried to read last night, or how much I tried to write in my journal. Nothing quelled the memory of what had occurred at the hotel gala. Eventually, I had passed into a heavy, dreamless sleep...and had only awoken at the crash of whatever was happening downstairs.

Out on the stairwell, I caught Jo, who ascended as I came to the banister.

"Don't bother going down there," she said, shaking her head. "You will regret it if you do."

"What's happened?" I asked as she swept past me.

"The stock market," she said. "Apparently, everyone's in a panic, trying to sell their assets as quickly as they can."

"Why?" I asked, turning to follow after her.

"No one seems to know, other than it's the natural thing to finally happen, isn't it? Stocks have been in decline for some time now," she said. "Evidently, things have suddenly hit bottom."

My stomach felt queasy. "Father thought this was inevitable?"

"I think he has been lying to himself if he really believed it would never happen," she said. She turned around halfway down the hall, hands planted on her hips. "He's trying to unload his investments as quickly as he can. He's been on the telephone all morning, trying to beat everyone else to it, and there have been advisors in and out the door every ten minutes for the last two hours."

"But if he sells and everyone else sells, too..." I began.

She nodded. "Exactly. There will be no money left in the market, and the price of everything and therefore the value of everything, will bottom out. He's trying to salvage what he can, but...."

"But we could lose everything," I finished for her.

She nodded, her expression grim. "Yes, we could. We should prepare for as much." She said nothing more as she turned and made her way to the end of the hall, to her room across from my own. She closed the door behind herself, shutting me away.

I stood there, alone in the middle of the hallway. It was clear she wanted nothing more to do with me, and I had no desire to make my way down into the chaos that was surely occurring. I didn't want to be in Father's way, nor did I want to trouble him any further.

But what about Uncle Walter?

Downstairs, a telephone rang out once, before growing silent again. Father must have answered immediately. The chime of the doorbell echoed and was soon followed by the sound of the front door opening.

I reached up and clutched the tiny silver key on the chain I wore around my neck, spinning it between my fingers.

I made my way back to my bedroom, certain I could not withstand the tide of motion downstairs. My stomach rumbled, though, despite the tension pressing in around me. When had I eaten last? At the gala the night before.

Was that only last night? It felt like days ago.

I rang the small golden bell just inside my door and went to my writing desk to wait. It wasn't long before I heard the soft *knock knock* on the door.

"Come in," I said, turning on the tufted stool.

Mrs. Riley, the head housekeeper, stepped into the

room. She had donned the same grey dress she always wore, paired with the ivory apron she somehow kept spotless despite the amount of backbreaking work she did around the house. Her thin lips curved into a faint smile as she inclined her head, her auburn hair tied in a tight bun at the back of her neck. "Good morning, Miss," she said. "What can I do for you?"

I resisted the urge to assault her with questions about my father. "I...I am not feeling terribly well this morning. I would like something small for breakfast in my room here."

"Certainly," she said. She didn't move, however, continuing to fix me with her grey eyes, the same shade as her dress.

I reached up to check my face; was there something there that she was staring at so intently?

"Is that all, Miss?" she asked. "Is there nothing else you need?"

"No, there is nothing I – " I stopped. In fact, there was a great deal I needed help with. However, what I found myself needing most was information. I swallowed, my lips dry. "It seems...awfully busy this morning."

It was more of a statement than a question, but she nodded. "You are worried about your father," she said. "The news we're hearing does seem distressing. But I would not trouble yourself with it too much, Miss. It will all work out, I'm sure."

I nodded, but her words brought little comfort.

"Your mother told me what happened last night," she went on. "About your uncle, I mean. It's a real shame, if you don't mind my saying so. He was such a kind man and treated all of the staff well."

"Thank you," I said, clearing my throat of a sudden tightness.

"I shall bring up your breakfast," she said. "Would you care for coffee, as well? It was roasted fresh, just this morning."

"That would be lovely, yes," I said.

She dipped into a slight curtsy and then left the room.

Only when she was gone did I allow myself to think again of the events of the previous evening. Sorrow, worry, and not least of all, anger washed over me. What, exactly, had happened to my uncle, causing him to die the way he had? It was a question that still had no answer and, for the first time, it occurred to me that perhaps it never would. At least, no answer that I would ever learn.

Mrs. Riley returned almost half an hour later, apologizing for the delay. She didn't need to explain that my father had wrangled some of the kitchen staff to tend to his errands for him, slowing the breakfast preparation. Nevertheless, she ensured that the small meal she'd brought up was satisfying and comforting. I even noticed a small teacake she had brought, decorated with almonds and candied ginger, my favorite combination.

"I'm sorry to trouble you, Miss Sylvia, but it seems there is someone here to meet with you," she said, setting the breakfast tray down in front of me. "He said you told him to be here this morning?"

I blinked up at her, my mind working frantically, but all I could think of was Uncle Walter. "I am not expecting anyone. What did he look like?"

"Tall, blonde, not a great deal older than you," she said. "I thought he might be another one of Miss Joan's gentlemen friends."

I frowned, picking up the teacake. "No, that doesn't sound like any of Jo's regulars. Anyway, I cannot think why anyone like that would wish to see *me* – "

My hold on the teacake tightened suddenly, squishing some of the delicate cake to crumbs that scattered across my writing desk.

"Oh, dear..." I said, remembering the man in the alleyway the night before. How had I forgotten?

It's easy to see why, between Uncle Walter's death and looming financial disaster.

I stood, wiping the crumbs from my blouse. "Did you invite him in?" I asked.

"He is waiting for you down in the drawing room," she said. "I made sure to keep him out of the way."

"Good. If it is who I think it is, then he is here about the open positions on our household staff," I said. "I have an idea he could be our next chauffeur or butler. Possibly both."

She nodded approvingly. "Well, as of right now, I think he would make a fine choice," she said. "Far better than the lout that applied most recently."

My brow furrowed. I knew the last applicant had been a poor choice but what made her think this stranger off the street, dirty and unkempt, would be better? Already I was questioning my own snap decision to trust him last night.

"May I also ask him a few questions after you have finished interviewing him?" she asked. "If I am to work alongside him, I should like to see if we would be able to create a more cohesive schedule for the rest of the staff. They have gone far too long without a proper hierarchy."

"Of course," I said, rising to my feet. "I will go down to him now, and I would like coffee served in the parlor."

She nodded and scurried away.

I finished the remains of my teacake and headed downstairs only moments later.

I hesitated for a brief moment outside the parlor, just narrowly missing Frank Morrow, who must have come by to meet with Father. He was intent on scrawling something down in a notepad as he hurried down the hall, so I decided it was best not to interrupt him. I had a task of my own to focus on.

I wondered now if I had made a foolish mistake last night. What had come over me to all but offer the job to a stranger, allowing him to waltz right into our house without knowing a thing about him? It was the utmost in stupidity. I was entirely unaware of who he was or what sort of past he had.

It isn't as if you know any of this about anyone else before they are hired, I reminded myself.

Yes, that was true...but the sort we usually employed had not been wandering the streets the night before in tattered garments.

If Father wasn't so preoccupied, he was sure to have been furious at my hiring someone he would likely not have chosen himself.

I drew in a sharp breath, inflating my confidence as much as I could. After all, if this person turned out to be unsuitable beneath the broad light of day, I could always reconsider the arrangement.

A man stood near the fireplace, still and serene. He looked up as I entered...and I stopped just over the threshold.

The man who stood there, smiling genteelly at me, was not the same one I had met the night before. His hair had been brushed back, the ends curling around his ears and the nape of his neck. He had sharp features, a wide jaw, and deeply set eyes which were a brilliant bottle green.

I remember those eyes.

"Ah, Miss Shipman," he said in a clear, British accent. "What a pleasure it is to see you again."

I blinked. I certainly recognized the voice.

He grinned, looking down at himself, and brushed the sleeve of his midnight blue suit, shaking it out. "I can see you are as astonished as I was upon my transformation. It's amazing what a good shave and a wash will do."

"Miles...is it?" I asked, as if I still needed to confirm it.

"Indeed," he said. "I am honored that you remembered."

It was astounding just how different he was from when I had met him the night before. If it were not for his voice and eyes, I would have assumed the man I met had passed my information on to some stranger in his stead. It seemed, however, that it was him.

Who was he, exactly? How in the world had he gotten himself cleaned up so quickly? A new suit, freshly shaved face, clean hair... How? *Unless the man on the street was nothing more than a façade?*

A shout in the hall behind me startled me, and I turned to glare at the door. More of Father's financial advisors, no doubt.

"I apologize that you are meeting with me today..." I said, turning back to Miles. "If my father was not otherwise occupied this morning, I know he would have preferred to be the one to speak with you."

Miles nodded his head. "I have heard rumors this morning of terrible losses having taken place overnight," he said. "I imagine your father is tending to those matters?"

"Yes," I said, seeing no reason to avoid the question. If he was to work for my family, then he may very well end up knowing more than I about my father's fortunes. "It seems there is a great deal of concern in the air, as of now."

"Yes, I noticed the extra activity in the streets, especially outside the banks," he said. "We may be heading for troubled times. Which leads me to ask...are you certain this would be a wise time for your family to hire a new member of staff?"

I hesitated. I had known in the back of my mind that the woes Father currently endured could very well affect our way of living...but it had not registered until now that it might even make it difficult to pay our staff or continue running our household.

I swallowed hard but refused to dwell on the problem until absolutely necessary. Until we knew more about what was happening, it seemed best to continue everything as usual, including the management of the house.

Besides, Mr. Morrow's words from the night before bounced to the forefront of my mind; "*And especially in these times, having loyal help may prove to be worth more now than ever.*"

"No, it is no trouble," I said. "I received some wise words of advice yesterday, which have helped me realize that while my father struggles to navigate these difficult times, it may as well fall on my shoulders to secure suitable help to maintain the affairs of the household."

He dipped his head. "Perfectly reasonable. And I would do all in my power to serve your family well. It would be my honor to be the first to rise and the last to bed, taking care of all that needed doing in the hours between."

"You would have a predecessor that was well liked by everyone in the house," I warned him. "Theodore is a name you will likely hear often, as he served us for years. If I know my mother's attachment to familiar people and things, nothing you do will ever be quite as good as if Theodore had done it."

He smiled. "I do not mind the challenge. I don't wish to be seen as trying to surpass the deceased but I shall do my best to live up to his memory, if I am the one you choose to bring in."

"I never said he had died," I said, my brow furrowing. ...*Did I?*

His smile faded ever so slightly. "I am sorry. I did not mean to presume out of turn."

"No...it's all right," I said, eyeing him more sharply. "It is just surprising that you guessed. But you are correct... There will be expectations placed upon you, some justified, others likely not. It will be difficult to impress both my family and the heads of the staff here."

"I would expect nothing less," he said agreeably. "And you needn't worry that I will find any of the work beneath me. I am just as happy to serve tea as I am to muck out stables." He looked around with a bemused grin. "Not that I shall have to concern myself with that here, will I?"

I gave him a small smile. "Well, perhaps not here, no, but my family's country estate has a handsome stable – " I stopped, realizing how needless it was to throw around information the way I was. "These are all things that will only be of concern to you if you are hired."

He nodded. "Fair point."

I regarded him with a scrutinizing gaze. He was quite young to be applying for the position but I couldn't refuse it to him for that.

Will this be strange for Joan and me, though? To have a butler and driver only a little older than the two of us? I wondered. *No, I suppose it won't be. I imagine it won't be long before she and I are both married and gone, and Father could certainly do with a man still in possession of his youth to get things done for him.*

"What hour do you rise in the morning?" I asked.

"As early as I am needed," he said. "Typically,

between five and a quarter after. If your father would need me sooner, however, I would have no trouble."

"Occasionally, you may be asked to take down notes for my father," I said. "How is your penmanship?"

"Good, if I might say so," he said. "I spent six months at Oxford learning to improve both my language and my writing style. I tend to be a bit wordy."

I raised my eyebrows. "Then you are very literate?" I asked.

"I suppose we might have different definitions of that," he said. "Homer? Plato? Aristotle?"

"Yes," I said, my brow furrowing. "You are well read, Mr. Miles."

"Please, as I said last night, it's just Miles," he said.

"Some might think such an educated man overqualified for the position," I said.

It was more a question than a statement but he sidestepped it easily.

"Well, can one ever really be too qualified for anything?" he asked, his smile faltering only a little.

"Perhaps not but it does seem odd..." I said.

He didn't respond to that, and I decided it would be unfair to pry into his background. I had found him on the city streets, after all, so he had clearly come down in the world. There was no need to embarrass him by asking for the details.

I changed the subject. "And how would you handle innocuous conversation?" I asked, thinking of Mother's gossiping rants and Joan's lengthy, descriptive tales.

"It troubles me not in the least," he said. "Though, it would not be my place to engage in such conversations. I shall simply be in the background, occupied by my tasks."

"How do you feel about cats?" I asked. "My mother has three."

"I grew up with barn cats," he said with a wry grin. "They loved when I brought them the last of my mother's knitting yarn to play with."

"And how good are you with keeping secrets?" I asked.

His face fell a bit, and I could plainly see that he understood the seriousness of my question.

"My father is an important man in this city," I said. "He has access to information many would want and some might try to steal. How do we know we can trust you?"

"Well..." he said, knotting his hands together, bowing his head. "I suppose there is nothing I could say that would rightly convince you, as you do not know if I am a man of my word. Just know that I understand the value of privacy and what happens when trust is betrayed." A storm flashed in his eyes.

I heard a deeper emotion in his voice than I had expected to; conviction. Something had hurt him or someone he loved, and he had developed a sort of bitterness about it. That might be for the best, mightn't it? If he knew what it was like, he might be less likely to betray my family and me. There was no better quality for a servant than loyalty.

I nodded, twirling my tiny silver key necklace. "Very well," I said. "I see no obvious reason not to give you a chance. I shall have Mrs. Riley, our head housekeeper, take over with the next portion of the interview. She will explain the duties involved in the role you would occupy in this house. Thank you for your time, Miles. It has been most interesting."

I turned to go.

"One moment, if I may, Miss Shipman..." he said.

I glanced at him over my shoulder. "Yes?"

"I wish you to know that I did put out feelers among my friends on the streets last night. While I have no information immediately ready, I will let you know what I learn of that person you were chasing near the hotel."

My mind reeled as I thought back to last night in that cold, dark alleyway. *Before I learned everything I did about Uncle Walter.* I licked my lips. "Yes, well...thank you."

"Unless you would rather I drop the matter?" he asked. "I can see my bringing it up is making you uncomfortable. I apologize for that. I had no idea."

"No...it's all right," I said, turning back around to

face him. I had nearly forgotten about the fleeing man. In the chaos of everything that happened last night, it was easy to see how it could have slipped my mind.

But if he had something to do with Uncle Walter's death...

"I would like you to discover what you can about that person," I said. "The man who died last night was my uncle."

His face fell. "Allow me to express my condolences," he said. "How very trying this time must be for your family."

"I appreciate your kindness," I said.

"I will do my best," he said. "This matter is now quite personal, and I can understand your desire to find this person who may have had some hand in whatever happened."

It troubled me to think anyone could have intentionally hurt Uncle Walter, could have made the choice to deliberately push him over that railing.

"I shall send Mrs. Riley in," I said, looking away, my composure in danger of crumbling. "Thank you again for your time, Miles."

And thank you even more if you can help me uncover what happened to my uncle...

5

The interview with Miles had surprised me for more than just how he had cleaned up. His last words about the man who had disappeared down the fire escape opened up an entirely new trail in my thoughts, one that I continually went back to as the day wore on.

Mrs. Riley seemed impressed enough with Miles, for by the time Jo, Mother, and I sat down to lunch – Father had rushed to the bank with Mr. Morrow to salvage what they could of a particularly steep investment – I saw Miles being shown around, instructed by her and one of the other servants.

"Who was that man?" Mother asked after they'd departed.

"Our new butler and driver," I said, not looking up from my plate of salad and chicken. I had hardly touched it, pushing it around with the end of my fork.

"Butler?" Jo asked. "How do you know?"

"Oh, finally," Mother said. "How wonderful to have found one at last. What did your father say of him?"

"He hasn't met him yet," I said.

"But when did he start? This morning?" Mother asked.

"He must have," Jo said, and I could feel her gaze on the top of my head, boring into my skull, willing me to look up at her. "I didn't see him around yesterday at all."

"I suppose I wouldn't have noticed, with the gala and all," Mother said. "My, won't it be nice to have a butler around again? Poor Mrs. Riley has been taking care of so much for us in Theodore's absence. I do hope she likes the new one. She must, having agreed to hire him. I suppose your father told her to just choose someone. It is really about time, isn't it? That will give your father a great deal of peace of mind."

"That is certainly my hope, too," I said.

Jo said nothing else through the duration of the meal, and I departed soon after to make my way up to my own room. I could not think with Mother's prattling on and Jo's furious stares at me across the table. My sister clearly knew I was keeping something to myself, something I didn't care to share with the rest of the family.

I would eventually have to admit how Miles had come to work here, but for now, I needed to think about what he had said to me. For some reason, that felt more pressing.

I closed the door to my room, locking it. I didn't want Jo barging in, demanding to know more about Miles and his sudden appearance. Going to the window, I stared out into the grey day.

People scurried along on the sidewalk below, which may not have been much different than usual, but I knew that many of them, like Father, were desperately worried. The whole city had likely begun to feel the depth of what had happened on Wall Street that morning.

Uncle Walter had made a great deal of his wealth from various investments, much like my father. Even last night, he had been discussing financial matters with Father, Mr. Morrow, and others of their friends. There had been a great deal of pretending that everything was well and good but I could tell concern had been eating away at them all. It was plain in their faces.

I frowned at the window, barely able to make out my own reflection in the bright glare of the glass. Uncle Walter fell last night...and the market crashed this morning.

Was it possible the two things were connected? Had he known his financial ruin was around the corner and not wished to face it?

An equally dark thought followed. Had someone else known, someone with a grievance against Uncle Walter, and hoped the chaos soon to follow would wipe all thoughts of his death from everyone's minds? In a way, the eve of disaster was the perfect time to commit a crime...

I thought back to Mother's words in the drawing room the night before. As intoxicated as she might have been, a stark truth had spilled out of her mouth; *"All I know is this isn't the first time we've lost relatives because of money...and it certainly will not be the last."*

My uncle falling to his death. The man fleeing the scene shortly after he fell. The crashing markets this morning.

My pulse pounded in my ears, a sickly rhythm that made my head spin.

It might as well have been a jigsaw puzzle dumped onto a table. The pieces lay scattered, each seemingly different, but some of the pieces must fit.

What if his death did have something to do with the rest of it?

I loathed the idea that he might have been pushed over that rail. If true, it would mean his death was no accident. He was killed.

A terrible chill raced down my spine.

Murdered.

Was that really what had happened?

My head ached, my heart running like a train off its

tracks. Did Father consider this? Had the police? Was I the only one who cared at all about any of it?

It certainly felt that way.

I noticed a car pull up outside the house. Almost immediately, one of its doors flew open and Father climbed out. I watched as he rushed up the front steps and into the house.

"I cannot stay here a moment longer..." I muttered, tugging the drapes closed.

I didn't want to see Father or hear how horrendous the day was going. I didn't want to sit and listen to Mother's pointless jabbering about everything that had nothing to do with Uncle Walter's death. I didn't want to wait for Joan to descend on me like a hungry shark smelling blood in the water, wanting to know everything about Miles and the reason for his sudden appearance.

I didn't want...any of it.

I grabbed a coat and rushed out into the cold, late October air.

The frantic noise of honking car horns rent the skies, echoing off buildings several streets over. I heard shouts, slamming doors, sirens blaring.

I didn't linger on the doorstep, but started down through Sutton Place, heading south. The bridge to the north was sure to be clogged with people trying to get both in and out of the city. While I typically loved the chance to walk over the East River, I knew today it would bring me no peace of mind.

And so I wandered. I allowed my feet to carry me to a familiar place, knowing that I would not wind up too far from home. The city might have been big, and ever growing, but I knew this corner of it like the back of my hand, having wandered through it so many times.

The whole world seemed burdened beneath a blanket of woe as I walked along. I could not find a single soul out enjoying themselves. The woman who always sold flowers on the corner of the street parallel to our house was absent. The blinds in the jeweler's shop had been drawn. I didn't see hide nor hair of the friendly beagle named Fritz that lived at number sixteen.

Everything really had been turned upside down.

I wandered and wandered...until I realized where my heart was leading me. A wicked thing, the heart. Its desires never did me any good. In my mind, I *knew* that my destination was a bad idea, but I still *wanted* to go. I had to. The compulsion to go, and just to look, over-whelmed my other senses.

I had to find out. I had to know for myself.

There might be nothing left to find...but even so...

It was not more than half an hour later that I found myself standing out in front of the Vandegrift Hotel. It was far sooner than I had ever expected to return, considering how I had sworn to myself mere hours ago that I would never set foot in that wretched place again.

Yet, here I was…striding in through the front doors, my heart lodged in my throat.

Most of the tables had been taken down and rolled away. A few that remained lay against the wall of windows, stripped bare of their pristine linen cloths. Chairs were stacked six high in a neat row beside them. A member of the hotel staff was nearby, on his hands and knees, scrubbing at something on the floor. A soapy bucket stood beside him, some of the suds pooling beneath it.

Another member of the staff swept the stairs, while another four stood in the dead center of the room, trying to repair some rather nasty damage to the marble tiles.

I shivered. *Where Uncle Walter hit the table and it broke beneath him.*

"Sorry, Miss, hotel's closed."

I turned to see a young man, dressed in the same uniform as the others, leaning on a broom near the other main door. His eyes were puffy but his expression was indifferent.

"I am not looking to stay here," I said, taking a step toward him. "But is the closure…because of anything in particular?"

The boy shrugged, brushing his dark hair from his

eyes. "Who knows? I was just told to turn away anyone who tried to come in here."

"I see," I said, eyeing the eerily round crack that ran through all the tiles, roughly the same size as the table had been. "I'm sorry. I was here last night, when a man – well, he – "

"Fell?" offered the young man. "Or threw himself over."

I blanched. "Threw himself over?"

He nodded. "That's what I heard."

That couldn't be true, could it? I wondered.

I swallowed. "I came to see...he was my uncle, and – "

"You really aren't supposed to be here," he said.

I stared at him, my worry growing, chewing at my insides. "Could I not have a moment to..."

"What? Pay your respects?" he asked. "Fine. But make it quick."

He reached out and snapped his fingers, drawing the attention of the other staff. The four gathered around the tiles made their way over to him.

"This girl is a niece of the man who died," he said, plainly. "Give her a few minutes to look around."

Another young man, perhaps no older than Joan, eyed me warily as if I might sprout a second head.

"Sorry for your loss," said a kind faced girl with her hair pinned up in a braid.

I nodded, and started over toward the tiles.

The young man I had first spoken with started to give them directions of what to do, while I lingered over the tiles, his droning voice making it hard for me to concentrate on the floor.

It was difficult to look at, far more difficult than I thought it might be. Knowing that Uncle Walter had fallen from so high above...

I did my best to look objectively at the floor. However, there was nothing there that told me anything useful.

I turned to look up at row after row of banisters, all stacked one on another in a perfect oval, all the way up twelve stories. I had seen people leaning over those golden railings all night last night, admiring the view of the foyer so far below.

Uncle Walter had been staying on the tenth floor, so it was reasonable to think that he had fallen ten stories.

My stomach twisted but I tried not to let my emotions distract me.

This would not help, I realized. The marble tiles would not miraculously speak and give me the answers I wanted. No, what I needed was to know what happened *before* he fell.

I looked up again.

The only way I would find that out was if I went and looked about in the room where he had been staying.

Was it possible his belongings would still be there, waiting for someone in the family to come and retrieve them? It was a small hope but a hope nevertheless.

I glanced at the workers. They had made themselves scarce; one had begun the task of cleaning the sconces along the wall. Another had joined the boy with the soapy bucket. The girl who had offered her condolences had busied herself with moving some of the vases filled with flowers and golden ribbon off their pedestals and tables.

I would only have one chance to look.

And if someone catches you? What are you going to do? I asked myself.

I hesitated, keeping my gaze fixed on the floor.

I will just explain that I am family, and – and – I'll burst into tears if I have to.

A bit extreme perhaps but I would do what I must.

Slowly, I started toward the staircase. Careful not to make any noise, watching each footstep, I began to climb the stairs, keeping myself low and hunched over.

With sweating palms and a thundering heart, I made it to the top of the first floor. I caught a glimpse of another hotel staff member down one of the long halls lined with rooms, and so darted around to the next staircase, far less grand that the one in the foyer, and hurried up and up and up.

I reached the tenth floor without incident, though not without having to clamp my hands over my mouth when my elbow banged into the end of the railing, where the metal bracket wrapped around the wooden bar. I sat down, breathing through my nose, willing the pain to pass, biting down on my tongue to counteract the pinpoint pressure in my arm.

It eased after a few moments, and I sat there for a bit, trying to catch my breath.

This floor seemed entirely vacant. I hadn't seen a soul for three floors. Either the rooms higher in the hotel had been cleaned, or no one dared come near.

I hoped, in a twisted way, that it was the latter.

I looked around, spotting a brass plaque on the wall inscribed with room numbers. Uncle Walter had been gracious enough to allow us up to see the room he was staying in, so that we might admire the luxuriousness of it. We had all been eager to see the newly designed rooms, said to be spacious and lush, decorated in only the finest of silks, velvets, and linens. I had found myself rather drawn to a suede armchair in olive green.

What room was it? 1024? Or 1042?

I couldn't decide.

Thankfully, they were down the same hall and I would pass by one before seeing the other. I hoped something would jog my memory as I wandered that way.

It seemed that the gap in my memory mattered little, as a note had been stuck to the door of 1024. My heart skipped as I noticed it. I hurried to the door and saw that the messy scrawl must have been written in a hurry.

We have been instructed not to disturb the contents of this room until the police have returned to collect evidence. Please refrain from entering until otherwise notified.

I tried the door handle and was surprised to find that it opened easily. Perhaps hotel employees had thought the note sufficient to keep anyone out.

I slipped inside, slowly shutting the door behind me with as little sound as possible. I winced as the latch slid into place, the metal clacking against itself.

My heart sank as I turned to look over the space. My uncle's suit coat lay on the end of the bed, as if it had just moments ago been tossed there. His suitcase rested open on the bench at the foot of the bed, with his clothes neatly packed inside. A carafe was on a low table beside the door, with a half-finished cup of coffee beside it.

Sorrow gripped my throat, but again, I would not be distracted.

There had to be something in here, more than his belongings. If his death had any such importance as I thought it might, then there would have to be some indication, somewhere.

What would that look like? I thought. *What should I be looking for?*

I might have been close to my uncle but that didn't

mean I would be able to tell if something belonged to him or not. I would not have known every one of his possessions. There could have been some sort of evidence staring me in the face in the form of a hat, or perhaps a glove, that would indicate someone else had been in here that night.

But none of that helps anyway, as our entire family came up to see this room, I thought. *He may have invited other friends to come up, as well.*

If not something belonging to someone else...then what?

I lingered near the door, my confidence diminishing with each passing second, like sand trickling through an hourglass. Why did I think I should come here in the first place? I didn't know the first thing to look for.

I drew in a deep breath and tried to push past the doubts.

The best way to start was just to look, so that was what I did.

Careful not to touch anything, even with the tip of my shoe, I started around the room, examining every surface and every item. Apart from the ache in my heart at seeing the way my uncle had left the last of his things, I tried to discern what I could about their placement and if there might have been anything strange about it.

I noticed he had left a newspaper lying on the

nightstand. I didn't dare touch it but wondered if there could have been anything of note in its pages.

A letter addressed to Jocelyn peeked out from the mesh lining of his suitcase. Could that be important?

I glanced at his suit coat lying on the bed, knowing the inner pockets were typically where my father put important items he wished to keep close to his person.

There may very well have been clues all around, but fearing touching anything, I resisted the urge to look. The last thing I needed was to disturb any sort of evidence that might be useful to the police later.

It was about that time that I reached a small writing desk in the corner, which had been blocked by the large armoire along the wall nearest the door. A couple of envelopes, sealed and stamped, lay in an untidy pile...but so did an open letter.

The pen lay beside it, likely the one used to write it.

I rushed over, grateful to have found something that might be of use, and began to read.

I can no longer bear the burdens so heavily laid upon me. The knowledge that has befallen me is too much, and I know that come morning, I shall be a ruined man. I trust the source who shared this information with me. I have reaped what I have sown, my heavy borrowing and specu-lating will leave me with nothing, and I cannot suffer the shame of being destitute. I am sorry, to all my loved ones, but you must understand that I simply cannot face it.

My gaze lingered on the last few sentences for what

could have been hours; time meant little when the repercussions of what had been written settled around me like sediment in a churned pond.

...I simply cannot face it.

In my mind, I saw Uncle Walter smiling at me over his violin in our parlor, as he and I played a duet for our families. I saw him laughing with my father as they stood out on the veranda at his own home, the stars twinkling behind them. I saw him just the night before, grinning at me after mentioning his newest violin purchase – a handsome piece made for him by a friend down in Pennsylvania – and how he couldn't wait for me to see it.

My mouth went dry. That man and the one who had written this note...they simply could not have been one and the same.

I read the letter again and my doubts increased.

Something doesn't look quite right...

I examined the writing, the words more than the meaning of the note.

I had written to and received letters from Uncle Walter many times in my life. His handwriting looked a great deal like my father's, given their similar instruction as children, but this letter was different.

I leaned closer, confirming my suspicions.

The way my uncle shaped his "A" and his "G" were quite different than what I saw here. There were more loops in the way my uncle wrote, and my father, as well. Why would he have changed his handwriting for this letter?

Unless –

Voices out in the hall made my insides go numb, as if I'd swallowed a bucket of icy water. I ducked against the wall, my heart pounding.

"...Sure we can't go in?" asked a male voice.

"That's what the note says," said another, also male but brighter in tone.

"Weren't the police here just this morning?" asked the first. "Have you checked with Robert to see if this note is old now?"

"I guess it shouldn't be an issue," said the second. "I'll go speak with him. Wait here until then, all right?"

"Aren't you even the least bit curious?" asked the first voice. "To see what he might have left behind?"

I looked around wildly. I would need to hide somewhere! But where? The armoire was the biggest piece of furniture in the room. I hurried to it, throwing open the door, and finding to my dismay a trio of shelves inside. There would be no way I could fit.

I closed it, wondering where in the world I would be able to go. I couldn't go through the door I came in, with those people just outside. Under the bed? I hurried over and lifted the duvet...but there was no opening beneath the bed. It had been blocked off by a solid bedframe.

"I guess I have been curious," said the second

person. "But that doesn't mean we should give in to the temptation."

"Why not?" asked the first.

I was running out of time.

What should I do? What should I do?

My eyes fell on the window...and the fire escape outside.

I snatched the letter from the desk, folding it as I turned away.

Then I hurried to the window, sliding the latch on the lock. I flinched as it smacked against the glass, but quickly threw it open. I was able to slip out onto the fire escape and push the window shut behind me. The latch would remain unlocked but I hoped they wouldn't notice, at least not until I was far enough away.

The world swirled beneath me as I looked over the side of the fire escape. Somehow, in my frantic need to escape, I had forgotten that I was all the way up on the tenth floor.

I grabbed hold of the metal railing, my knees buckling. I pinched my eyes shut, willing my head to stop spinning.

I can't stay here. They'll see me out the window.

I urged myself toward the stairs, promising myself over and over that the farther I descended, and the more quickly, the better and safer I would be. I needed no urging on and reached the bottom before I lost my balance again.

When I finally made the last leap from the bottom step, my knees gave way beneath me and I sank down onto the dirty alley pavement.

I drew in a deep breath, trying to calm my nerves. I was on the ground, out of that room, out of danger... If it had actually *been* danger. From the sounds of things, it had only been two nosy hotel employees I had fled. But I couldn't take the chance of them seeing me and reporting my presence to the police. Who knew what they would make of my trespassing?

My fist tightened around the letter in my hand and a small feeling of gratification rose up within me. At least I had this.

Was it really worth it, though?

I got to my feet and brushed my knees off. I turned to look up at the fire escape, and I staggered as the sky swayed. I shook my head, looking away. It was astonishing how high I had actually been.

That was when I realized that this might have been the same fire escape I had seen the man fleeing down. I turned and hurried back toward the doorway I had come out of last night, off the main foyer, and looked back over my shoulder at the fire escape.

That looks about right...

I looked down at the letter in my hand. Had that

someone been running from my uncle's room? And whoever it was...was he the one who wrote the note?

That didn't seem entirely impossible now, did it?

6

"Oh, Miss Sylvia. I hadn't even realized you had left."

Mrs. Riley happened to be passing through the foyer as I reentered the house.

"Oh – " I said, closing the door behind me. "I just...I just needed a walk."

It was true, in a way.

"Are you all right?" she asked, setting down the laundry basket in her arms and hurrying over to me. "You look as if you've had a fall." She looked down at my scuffed shoes and stained skirt.

"Yes..." I said. "I suppose I did, didn't I?"

Mrs. Riley furrowed her brow but withheld any questions she might have had about how I had fallen. "Be sure to leave that out for me to take care of for you. You don't want those stains to set in."

"Of course," I said, in a hurry to change the subject. "How is Miles settling in?"

She straightened, glancing over her shoulder. "It will take him time to get adjusted, but overall, I think he will prove to be a good addition to the household. With some training, of course." She nodded. "I told him that he was to be properly moved in by this time next week, to which he agreed."

"Has he been introduced to Father?" I asked.

"He has," Mrs. Riley said. She hesitated for a moment. "Given the troubling news of this morning, your father was quite distracted and didn't ask nearly as many questions as I expected him to." She sighed. "I suppose I should be grateful he trusts my judgment so thoroughly that he would leave this to me. And to you, of course, Miss Sylvia."

My heart quickened. "Did you tell Father I was the one who invited Miles here?" I asked.

"Well...no, I suppose that did not come up," Mrs. Riley said. "I shall make sure to inform him when I next – "

"Please don't," I interrupted. "I think it best that he believes you selected the new staff member. He might think it silly of me to interfere."

Mrs. Riley studied my face, her eyes sweeping over me as if I were a complicated tapestry. "Very well," she said. "If you prefer, of course we shall keep this all between us."

"Thank you," I said, folding my hands in front of me. The coolness of the letter tucked inside the sleeve of my blouse pressed against my skin as I moved. "Is my father home now?" I asked.

"No," Mrs. Riley said. "He's gone out again, with Mr. Morrow. It's the third time today."

"Has anything improved?" I asked. "Surely by now..."

"I would certainly hope so," she said, but no hope brightened her face. "However, given the anxious nature he has had, flying around here like a startled fox..." She shook her head, her perfect bun staying in place. "I do not know what to expect. It might be some time before we see a great deal of turn around."

Another knot of worry settled in my gut. I took hold of the silver key on my necklace once more, my eyes darting to the floor.

"I must be off, Miss," the housekeeper said, as if coming to her senses suddenly. She swept off down the hall. "Remember to lay that skirt out for me before you go to bed tonight."

"I will," I said, though she had already disappeared through the door to the kitchens.

Is this what life is to be like now? I wondered. *Am I to bear all these worries for...how long?*

First the concern surrounding our family's financial state. Then the dead man at the party last night, who ended up being Uncle Walter. Then finding the letter –

I needed to get the letter to a safer place. Keeping it on my person could not be a worse place for it. I reached into my sleeve, thinking I was fortunate it had not fallen out somewhere.

I started down the hall, and heard a shift of furniture coming from the second parlor off the main staircase. Much smaller than the one we typically received guests in, it had become more for personal family gatherings. Who would be in there at this hour? Surely Mother had settled herself with a drink in the drawing room that overlooked the back garden and the river, as she always did. Joan would be up in her room, as she always seemed to be, and Father –

Miles, his back to me, stood on the far side of the room, tossing a plain white sheet over the top of a wardrobe. It settled on the piece like gently falling snow.

He turned a moment later and offered a polite smile, on seeing me in the doorway.

"Hello, Miss Sylvia," he said.

"Miles," I said. "I'm sorry if I interrupted. What is it you're doing?"

He glanced up at the now covered wardrobe. "Your father has instructed me to prepare some of these pieces of furniture for sale," he said, laying his hand against the sheet and patting it as if it were a horse.

"For sale?" I asked, blanching. I stared around at the half dozen pieces of furniture that had been covered. "All of these?"

Miles nodded. "Unfortunately, yes."

"But why?" I asked, stepping into the room. "Some of these pieces have been in our family for generations now."

Miles moved aside as I examined the furnishings. "I did not ask. I did not think it my place."

My jaw muscles clenched, and I shook my head. Was the situation truly so dire that my father feared we would need to begin selling our belongings to make money?

"You have a look about you, Miss," Miles said in a hushed voice. "A look that says you have been recently frightened."

I stiffened, partially turned away from him as I was. I could feel his bottle-green gaze upon my face, and wondered wildly how he could possibly have known that?

"Or perhaps...you are just trying to work something out," he added. "I noticed you stepped out for some time. May I ask if it had anything to do with your uncle?"

I rounded on him. Had I somehow spoken my thoughts out loud? I quickly reflected upon the conversation we had in the drawing room when he first arrived that morning, and could think of nothing that might have indicated I would be doing anything to personally pursue the matter. "How did you know?" I asked, before I had even considered if it was wise to admit to anything in the first place.

He gave a wry grin and started over to the other side of the wardrobe. He tugged on the sheet, attempting to straighten it so that it fully covered both sides. "I have learned a great deal about people," he said. "Including how to read them. It was clear on your face that something was troubling you. I don't suppose you meant to appear that way, and given how difficult the past few days have been for your family, it might be of little surprise. However, you demonstrated bravery last night, running out after that man who fled down the fire escape. And learning that he might have had something to do with your uncle's death..."

He stopped, and took a few steps toward me.

This close, I could see flecks of blue in those green eyes, especially around the outer iris.

"Perhaps I am overstepping my bounds, but I assume you have now taken this whole affair personally and have decided to take matters into your own hands..." His statement, which sounded more like a question, trailed off.

My throat went dry, and as I tried to swallow, it burned. Was I truly so easy to read? And if I was, who else might also read my intentions? "You are...quite forward," I said, my mind racing.

Yes, he was forward. Incredibly so...and yet, for some reason, I didn't feel terribly troubled by it. He had helped me last night without question, without even a thought, chasing someone down who might have easily turned on him to kill him just as my uncle had been killed. He had chosen to trust me, in a split second decision.

I found him trustworthy. I *wanted* to tell him, even if it was simply because he already knew something about what had happened the night before. The rest of my family had no idea that I had chased someone down the alley. The rest of my family had no idea that Uncle Walter might very possibly have been pushed to his death. And the note I had found would have likely cemented their opinion all the more that there was nothing to be done.

"I apologize if I am being too forward," he said. "I recognize the look on your face and I just wanted to make sure you are doing all right."

"I..." I began. I glanced over my shoulder at the open door and debated for only a moment before I went to close it.

His brows rose ever so slightly as I approached him again.

"I went to see the room where my uncle was staying," I confided. "At the hotel, I mean. To see if there was anything that might tell me who may have..." I couldn't bring myself to say it. Not yet.

I expected shock. I expected scrutiny. I expected an accusation, yet all he met me with was a simple nod. "And did you find anything?"

"You aren't surprised?" I asked. "I sneaked in, you see." Perhaps I had not made myself clear enough.

He nodded again. "I suppose the room had been blocked off by the police?"

"Yes," I said. How was he so calm about this?

"What did you find?" he asked.

With an unsteady hand, I reached into the sleeve of my blouse, and withdrew the letter. I handed it to him.

He took it, and I watched his eyes move over the words. "A suicide note," he said plainly. When he returned his attention to me, he wore a considering look. "But you must think it is a fake if you took it from the room."

"How do you know that?" I asked.

He handed the letter back to me. "If you hadn't found anything out of the ordinary, then you would have most likely left everything as it was. Why did you take the note?" he asked.

"As you said, I – I think it was written by someone else," I said. "The handwriting is different from his."

He said nothing, rubbing the side of his face as if massaging a sore tooth.

"I didn't know what to do," I said. "There were people standing outside the door, staff of the hotel waiting to come in and clean. They were daring one another to come in and look through my uncle's things, and I – I panicked, grabbing the letter."

My heart thundered as I looked down at it. "The police are sure to return, aren't they?" I asked. "What if they have been in there and seen it already, and when they return they see that it's missing?"

My stomach twisted at the thought. "I may very well have stolen evidence, crucial evidence, that could entirely change the outcome of their investigation," I said.

"The best thing you can do right now is not to panic," Miles said in a low voice, his eyes passing to the door. "And, if I may give you a bit of advice...not to give away every bit of information you know. Sometimes, there is such a thing as telling too much."

My face burned. He was right. Without thought, I had rattled off far more than he needed to know, far more than I needed to say.

"You need not worry about what you have told me, Miss Sylvia," Miles said. "I am not speaking of myself, but others. Those who might possibly be involved in this matter. If you allow them to know everything you do, then you shall have no advantage."

My disappointment flipped on its head almost at once. He wasn't telling me off; he was helping me.

I narrowed my eyes. "For a man just off the streets, turned household servant, you seem well versed in matters of secrecy," I observed.

Miles met my gaze and held it for a moment, as if weighing whether or not *he* could trust *me*. "I suppose the fairest way I can put it is that I understand what it means to be hurt...and I know the lengths a person will go to in order to satisfy their own ends. You must forgive me but I do not wish to say more than that."

The vague answer certainly left me hoping for more but I dared not press. Already he had given me more help than he needed to, advice as well.

"I have experience, not because I wanted to have it but because I had no choice but to obtain it," he went on. "If you wish to truly pursue the truth of this devastation that has fallen upon your family, then you must be prepared for the risks you will face. It is a dangerous road and you may not like what you find."

My stomach tightened uneasily.

"Are you truly ready to follow this?" he asked. "You still have a chance to back out. You can admit what you found to your father, allow him to follow through – "

"He won't do anything," I blurted out and immediately regretted it.

Miles stopped, too. "Evidence like that letter might change his mind," he said.

I shook my head, thinking back to what Father had said last night. "I think he is more concerned about his fortunes than the death of his brother."

Miles nodded, his expression somber. "I suppose I

understand why you are taking these matters into your own hands."

"I wouldn't be, not if I didn't feel as if I was the only one who cared about it in the first place," I admitted.

"That makes a great deal of sense," he said. "Well... you have in your hand there what I would consider substantial evidence written in that letter. You said it wasn't his handwriting?"

I nodded. "I could prove it easily, as well. I have many old letters from him, which this one could be compared to."

"Good," Miles said. "That's clever thinking." He moved to a stack of clean linens set neatly on the windowsill and unfolded the top one with a flick of his wrists. "Now for the difficult question. Who would your uncle have known that could have reason to do this to him?"

I blinked a few times, my mind suddenly blank. "I do not know," I said. "In truth, there must have been so much about him that I didn't know."

Miles carried the sheet over to one of my mother's armchairs, upholstered in an ugly canary yellow, and threw the sheet over it. "Yes, but if someone despised him, that would likely have been obvious. Or perhaps there was someone he had been having a difficult time with?"

I gave him a pointed look. "Do you have an idea?" I

asked. "It seems you might have more knowledge than I do at the moment."

He shrugged. "They say that when violent events occur, the crime is typically committed by someone the victim knows. It may be a mutual acquaintance that you know, as well." He straightened the sheet over the chair. He regarded it with a tilt of his head, and then shot me a small smile. "I suppose your mother shall be heartbroken over the loss of this chair?"

I glanced at it. "She may be," I said. "But none of the rest of us will be."

His smile grew as he turned away from it. "What of your uncle's family?" he asked. "Did he have a wife? Children?"

"Yes," I said. "He was married but his wife died a few years ago. He is older than my father, you see, and so my cousins are all much older than Joan and I, all grown and married."

Miles pulled another sheet from the pile. "And are you close to any of them?"

I shook my head. "No, I never was," I said. "I think Uncle Walter enjoyed spending time with Joan and me because he missed his own children being young and because I was one of the few people he could play violin duets with. I believe most of his children moved out west. He lived largely alone, and as such, he decided to remarry. Or at least, that was the plan, as he had a fiancé at the time he died."

"You said his previous wife died some time ago?" Miles asked. "How?"

"An illness," I said and then my eyes widened. "If you are wondering, she did not die at all in a similar way to my uncle."

Miles nodded. "Good to know. That was my next question. So he had little relationship with his children, his wife was gone...and you said he was engaged?"

"Yes," I said.

"Why hadn't they been married yet?" Miles asked.

I hesitated, considering.

"How long had they been engaged?" he asked.

"I...can't quite recall," I said. "Perhaps since last Christmas?"

"That's an unusually long delay for a second marriage. Why wouldn't they have been married much sooner?"

"I don't know," I said.

"What of their relationship?" Miles asked.

"Why are you asking so much about her?" I asked.

"As I said, it is often those closest to a person who kill them," Miles said. "So, what of the fiancé?"

I hesitated. Was I really going to consider this? To think that Jocelyn could have had something to do with her own fiancé's death? "It couldn't have been her," I thought with immense relief washing over me.

"It was a man I saw fleeing last night. You saw him. It couldn't have been her."

Miles carried the new cloth to a small, round table in the corner.

That hurt to see covered, as every season Mrs. Riley would set a new lovely vase atop it with bouquets of fresh flowers or sprigs of greens in the winter. A small touch but a spot of joy I had not realized I loved so much until it was now about to be gone.

"Unless the fiancé had an accomplice..." Miles said.

I shook my head. "I appreciate you being so willing to discuss this subject with me but I do not wish to accuse my acquaintances. I have no reason to think Jocelyn would have had anything to do with my uncle's death."

Miles paused in his work. "Are you sure about that? Your tone tells me there is something you don't wish to admit, even to yourself," he said. "They did not have the best relationship, did they?"

I opened my mouth to protest but I could not, with honesty, dispute his words. "She – " I stopped, guilt washing over me like a dark tide, pungent with rotting fish. "No, I'm sorry. I can't – "

I turned to walk toward the door and he didn't stop me.

I, however, did stop myself.

Licking my lips, I turned back to face him. He

waited patiently near the small table, as if he had known I would not walk out the door.

"I...I don't like this," I said. "Any of it. I don't want to accuse her of something so – so –" I still could not bring myself to say it.

"That's perfectly reasonable," he said. "No one wants to believe anyone in their family, or very nearly a part of, could be responsible for such a thing. Whenever you hear anything, it's always someone else's family, their brother, their cousin, their friend. We never think it could happen to us."

I nodded, eyeing the floor at my feet.

"She was acting rather strange that night," I said. "My mother had told me that the pair of them had been having trouble, that my uncle had even been considering severing the engagement."

Miles raised an eyebrow. "That sounds terribly suspicious," he said. "What was the cause of the trouble between them?"

"I have no idea," I said. "The whole situation was bizarre from the beginning. When he introduced her to us for the first time, we were all startled that she was so young. As young as I am, in fact. I know that isn't entirely unusual, but Joan stated the obvious that very night, after she left; all that woman wanted was a rich husband. Why else would she be marrying someone so much older than she?"

"Perhaps she had no other prospects," Miles said.

"Yes, but she is more than young enough to be his daughter," I said. "And given where she comes from..."

"But your mother said your uncle was looking to end the engagement?" Miles asked.

I nodded. "I overheard her telling some of her friends about it just a few days ago, and then she and I discussed it later."

He snapped his fingers. "*That* is the thread we should be tugging at, if we wish to unravel the truth. Now...all we need to do is speak with someone who would know this Jocelyn. Does she have friends or family in the area?"

"In a way..." I said.

"Not the most pleasant sort?" Miles asked.

I shook my head. "It's not exactly that. They're not the most socially acceptable sort. At least, not to families like mine."

"Even better," Miles said. "They sound like the ideal sources of information."

7

"I suppose I understand your reluctance now," Miles said, staring out the windshield of the motorcar as we idled outside of a tall unassuming brick building at the edge of the city. "I had not realized your uncle was planning to marry someone entirely out of his social sphere."

I glanced up at the sign swinging above the plain wooden door, which showed a silhouette of a rather shapely woman singing into a microphone with a saxophone player beside her. An old converted fish packing facility, the place had been purchased by a local mogul intent on entertaining the masses with cheap food and singing. "This is where the pair of them met, I gather," I said. "After my aunt's death, it seems my uncle was looking outside his usual habits to find some relief from his woes."

Miles nodded, and turned around to look at me. "Are you certain you want to pursue this?" he asked. "It is not too late to turn back."

I shook my head. "No. I have come this far, haven't I?" Since no one else wanted to find out what really happened to my uncle, who else would do it but I? And with Miles being willing to help, and seeming so conveniently experienced at uncovering information, there would never be a better opportunity.

"Very well," he said, putting the car in park and shutting off the engine. He came around to the back and helped me from the vehicle.

"You seem to be adjusting to your duties rather well," I said. "Even though today is only your first day."

He smiled as he shut the car door behind me. "I suppose this is the sort of job I was made for," he said. He glanced up at the building. "This jazz club is where she works, you said?"

I nodded.

"I cannot imagine your family being terribly thrilled about the idea," he said. "Of your uncle marrying her."

"No, we were not," I said. "My father especially made it clear that we cared nothing for this sort of life-style and the typical types of people it attracts."

Miles nodded. "Rather rough sort," he said. "He is right about that."

I sighed. "Nevertheless, we were hospitable

enough, as we had little choice," I said. "At least, we tried to be. I have tried to get to know her but she has made it difficult."

"And why is that?" he asked.

"My sister put it best," I said. "Joan always said that it seemed as if Jocelyn was trying to overcompensate for the life she was leaving behind, trying too hard to fit into the life she was stepping into."

"But she still works here?" Miles asked. "Why had she not left the job?"

I shrugged. "Perhaps she enjoys her independence or perhaps she was not quite in a position to go," I said. "She didn't yet have my uncle's full financial support, after all..."

Miles frowned. "Or there is something tying her to this place that she didn't want to leave behind," he said. "That possibility might be worth tucking in our back pocket. It could be part of the reason your uncle was considering breaking off the engagement."

"It could also be that she feared being left behind, unable to attain the wealth she wanted from my uncle," I said, allowing myself to voice my deepest fear.

He gave me a pointed look. "That's quite an observation."

"I always thought it was about nothing more than money for her, and if he broke the engagement off, then she would be deprived of that money," I admitted. "It makes me wonder if that's not why she was trying so hard to get him to move the wedding up sooner."

A gust of wind rushed down the long street, funneled in our direction between the buildings on either side. I shivered, wrapping my full-length fur coat more tightly around myself.

"Let's get you inside," Miles said, his hand hovering behind me, yet not quite touching my back as he escorted me up the crumbling steps to the door of the club.

The thick stench of stale smoke and cheap perfume wafted out as soon as Miles opened the door, as if it too had been struggling to escape. I nearly gagged on the potency of it, trying to gulp in any pocket of fresh air that might still be inside.

There wasn't any.

The club itself had been laid out on the floor of the old packing facility. The door opened onto the old cargo platform, where we found ourselves looking down into the rest of the club. Tables were scattered about on the cement floor and the stage had been retrofitted along the far wall, likely where barrels were once stacked for shipping. Lights had been hung from the ceiling, though haphazardly, and mismatched rugs had been thrown around on the floor to absorb the sound and brighten up the space.

A saxophone player stood on the stage, swaying as he played alongside a single snare drum player. I didn't recognize the song but I hardly recognized any jazz music. The stage held a baby grand piano, a cello, and a trio of chairs along the side, all of which were empty at the moment.

"Good afternoon. May I help you?"

We were intercepted by a tall, lanky boy who was most certainly younger than even Joan. He had a long face and large front teeth.

"Yes. We are looking for a woman called Jocelyn, who works here. Is she in?" Miles asked.

My heart began to race. We were really going to question her about this. Suddenly, it became all the more real to me.

The boy shook his head. "You would do better to come back later tonight, when she will be waitressing."

I blinked at him. "I'm sorry, did you say that Jocelyn would be waitressing?" I asked.

He looked at me, his forehead wrinkling. "Yes," he said.

"But I thought she was one of the singers?" I asked.

The boy shook his head. "You are talking about Jocelyn Parker?"

"Yes," I said.

"As far as I know, she has never performed here," the host said. "Would you still like a table? Or are you going to come back later when she is here?"

Miles looked at me, searching my face.

I didn't know what to think. She had been lying to us all along.

"I think we would still like a table," Miles said, staring out over the almost empty room. "You'll have to excuse the lady. She lost her uncle last night."

"I'm sorry to hear that," the boy said. "It's been a hard night on everyone, from what I have heard. Should I get you some coffee?"

"That would be excellent, thank you," Miles said.

The boy led us to a nearby table, seated near the long bar that butted up against an old tank. It seemed they used it for storage of their own, holding various items used by the employee who stood at the counter. I saw bottle after bottle of soda water, canned fruits, syrups, and a long row of pale green sundae glasses.

"Is there anything else you need?" the host asked.

"How well do you know Jocelyn?" I asked. *I feel as if I hardly know her at all now.*

"I've only been here for about a year," the boy said. "So I've worked with her for a while. Do you know her, too?"

"Only a little," I said, which felt fairly truthful at the moment.

The boy pointed to the man behind the counter, a tall fellow as wide as a refrigerator, all muscle and pointed cheekbones. "She and Henry are close," he said. "If you want to know anything about her, like when she might be in, you should ask him."

I perked up a bit, watching as the man filled the bottom of a sundae glass with some strawberry red syrup, topping it with the bubbling soda water.

"That will be all for now, thank you," Miles said.

The young host nodded and scurried away.

I looked at Miles. "She told us she was one of their most popular singers here," I said under my breath, glancing up at the stage in the corner. "To think she lied to us for all this time..."

"I suppose it might have been a matter of pride for her," Miles said. "A singer would certainly sound a little more reputable to your family than a server."

"What of the bartender?" I asked. "Do you think it would be wise to speak with him?"

"I do," Miles said. "If the pair of them are close, it makes me wonder if there is more going on between them than simple friendship."

"You think she was running around on my uncle?" I asked.

Miles shrugged. "Only one way to find out."

Together we walked toward the bar.

"I think I should talk to him alone," I said, pausing to hang back for just a moment.

"Why?" Miles asked.

"...I have an idea," I said.

"All right," Miles said. "I'll be nearby, if you need me."

It was foolish, I knew, but I found myself spurred

on by the pain of the past two days. Overwhelming emotions sloshed around inside me and all I wanted was a means by which I could expel them.

I stepped up to the counter, taking a seat at one of the bright red stools.

The employee's head swiveled around, his hand deftly poised over another glass as he filled it, this time with slices of orange and dark, syrupy cola. "Well, well," he said, a toothy grin spreading across his chiseled features. "It has been a long time since a young lady as pretty as you sidled up to my bar all on her own. Thought for sure that fella you walked in with belonged to you."

I returned the grin just as easily, laying my chin in my hand, resting my elbow casually on the bar. "No, he's only my chauffer but he's awful protective of me." I giggled.

He set the glass down on a tray, pushing it off to the side with an order sheet, and walked over to me. He laid his hands flat on the counter as he drank me in and his smile grew. "What's your name?"

"Mildred," I said, borrowing my mother's name. I fluttered my eyelashes at him. "And I hear they call you Henry."

He chuckled, swiping the rag from his shoulder to wipe down the countertop between us. "That's what I'm told," he said. "Can I get you anything to drink? I make a mean chocolate malt. Might bring some cheer after the tough morning we've all had."

"I'd love one," I said with a broad, glittering smile that Joan often used on the men she liked.

"Haven't seen you around here before," Henry said, deftly scooping a glass off the top of the tank behind him and sending it sliding down the bar to the ice box.

"Haven't been here," I said.

"Too bad," he said. "Though I guess you're here now, aren't you? How'd you hear about us?"

"Word of mouth," I said. "I have some family that knows this place."

"Always good to hear our reputation is preceding us," he said. He filled the glass with the malt, milk, and a scoop of the chocolate ice cream. He slid it down the bar, where it stopped perfectly in front of me. "There you are. A real treat."

"Thank you," I said, and gave it a try.

He came back to stand, watching me.

"Mmm, it's delicious," I said, and meant it. When was the last time I had enjoyed something so simple?

"I was hoping to catch Jocelyn," I said, turning to glance over my shoulder. "But she isn't here yet."

"No, not yet," he said. "That's all right, though. It isn't too busy now. Shouldn't be for a while. That'll give me plenty of time to give you my full attention."

"I heard the two of you are...close," I said, raising my eyebrows, swirling the spoon in my glass, the soft *tink* of the metal against the side the only sound for a moment or two.

He tossed the rag back over his shoulder, looking away as he gave a careless bat of his hand. "Eh, she and I aren't as familiar as people think. We've only been out together a few times." He leaned closer, his smile returning. "She's old news, anyway."

"Why is that?" I asked, tilting my head as innocently as I could to the side, hoping my wide eyes held no great concern, only mild curiosity.

His toothy grin only got wider. "It must be because you were about to walk into my life," he said.

I offered another giggle, partially covering my face with my hand.

He laughed along with me, apparently convinced by my reaction.

"Well, aren't you a forward one?" I said. "How am I to know you are telling me the truth?"

"I suppose you will just have to wait and see," he said jovially. "A little bit of mystery is good, in my opinion."

I smiled. "About Jocelyn..." I said. "I want to know why you call her old news when I have heard otherwise?"

His smile fell slightly and his brows drew toward one another. "She's getting married," he said. "She and I are history. You can be sure about that."

I pursed my lips. It was interesting to know she had told her friends here of her engagement.

"You certainly seem awfully concerned about her," he said, leaning down on his elbows on the bar, his grey eyes piercing me. "Are you and she friends?"

"Not really, no," I said, my face burning. My appetite vanished, and I pushed the cup away.

"What was it you needed to talk to Jocelyn about that was so important?" he asked.

I swallowed, my mind racing. I watched as my plan quickly began to unravel right before my eyes.

What would the harm be in telling him, really? Maybe he would be able to help. Maybe he would *want* to help, out of affection for her. I didn't need to let him think I was interested, not really. But maybe if it was for her wellbeing –

"Sylvia?" I heard from behind me, and I froze instantly. "What in the world are you doing here?"

8

I spun around on the barstool, already knowing who I was about to see.

Jocelyn stood just beside the bar, one foot already past it; she must have been lost in her own thoughts, only taking notice of me as she drew nearer. I wondered if she might have even recognized my voice. She gaped at me, her eyes narrowing as she looked back and forth between Henry and I.

"Oh, Jocelyn – hello," I said, sliding down off the barstool. I smoothed my hands over my coat. "I was just – "

"I heard my name mentioned. Why are the pair of you discussing me?" she demanded, striding over to us, the heels of her shoes clacking against the concrete floor.

"Oh, it was nothing," Henry said quickly. He pulled

the rag from his shoulder and started cleaning the counter again in long, lazy swipes.

"I'll deal with *you* later," she hissed, shooting him a look that could have melted steel. Then she reached out and grabbed hold of my wrist, dragging me away from the bar.

"Wait – Jocelyn. Hold on," I protested.

I looked around, my gaze sweeping the room until I spotted Miles sitting back at our table. His eyes widened when he saw me being led away, and he rose to follow, but I shook my head. Slowly, he lowered himself back into his seat.

Jocelyn dragged me to the mouth of a hallway off the main room. The clink of dishes told me I must have been standing near the kitchen.

She rounded on me, her eyes ablaze. "What are you doing here?" she asked through clenched teeth, her nostrils flaring.

"I – I came to see you," I said, my heart pounding in my ears. "I wanted to speak with you."

"And somehow decided that it was the right time to flippantly flirt with Henry?" she asked.

"No, I didn't – " I began, raising my hands in defense.

"I saw you," she said, her eyes lowering to slits like a cat's. "You should *not* get involved with that man."

I hesitated. It made me wonder how much of what Henry had told me was nothing more than sweet words. Then I remembered my uncle...and my blood began to simmer. "And what of my uncle?" I asked, glaring up at her, as she stood a few inches taller than me. "Are you and this Henry together?"

Jocelyn's jaw fell open and her cheeks flushed scarlet. "I – That isn't – that isn't any of your business," she snapped back.

"Oh, it isn't?" I asked, the anger pulsing through me, urging me on. "My uncle is gone, and I come here to learn that you and this Henry are as close as you are?"

"You think I didn't want to marry Walter?" she asked. "That I am not devastated by his – by his – " She floundered for the word. She then burst into tears, covering her face with her hands. Her sobs echoed down the hall, and out of the corner of my eye, I saw Henry's head swivel around to look for the source of the crying.

I took a step toward her. "You can pretend all you like," I said. "But everyone knows all you ever wanted was Uncle Walter's money. You never cared about him."

She stared at me, her eyes blazing with a hatred that I suspected had always been there. "How dare you?" she breathed.

"We all suspected it from the very beginning," I said, my voice rising in volume. "Why else would you decide to marry someone old enough to be your father? And all the talk about changing the wedding date, when he was considering ending the engagement? It all makes sense! He must have known you were after his money! And when he wouldn't move up the wedding..."

My head pounded, as I stared at her.

"You did it..." I whispered. Then the anger burst out of me. "*You* did this! You!"

"What do you mean?" she asked, drawing her eyebrows together. "What are you saying?"

"My uncle didn't fall," I said, my eyes flashing. "Someone pushed him!"

"You are accusing me of such a thing?" she asked. "How *dare* you! You think that I – "

"It's time to go, Miss Sylvia," said a low voice in my ear. Before I had the chance to protest, I found myself dragged away from Jocelyn by a strong hand in the crook of my arm. I wheeled around and found the back of Miles' head as he whisked me out of the hall and toward the door.

"Don't you come back here!" Jocelyn shouted after me. "Don't you ever come back!"

The anger spoiled in my stomach, like vinegar in milk. The strength sapped from my limbs as it sank in precisely what I had allowed to escape from my mouth. Nervous voices filled the room behind us, including Henry, who had hurried over to Jocelyn, asking what had happened. Jocelyn shrieked and sobbed in an outrage that may or may not have been genuine.

"That was close..." Miles said as he pushed open the door. With a quick, deft motion, he swept me out over the threshold and closed the door behind us.

I stood there on the stone steps and shivered as the brisk wind brushed against my cheeks.

"Come along," he said, not taking his hand from my arm, steering me down the stairs.

Regret sloshed around inside me, as I realized what a mess I had made of my little investigation. I had come here to question Jocelyn, not announce that I suspected her. I had made quite a scene in the process, as well. I couldn't remember the last time I had shouted at anybody in public. Joan was most likely the last victim of my temper, but even that had not been in front of so many people.

My face burned all the way to my neck, as I realized I had made an utter fool of myself...all over an assumption. All over a suspicion that I had absolutely no evidence to support.

I pinched my eyes tightly shut as Miles led me away from the jazz club. There was no telling how far word of this incident might spread. I would just be lucky if no one in my family heard of it.

It took far longer to reach the car than I wanted. I worried with each step that Jocelyn would race out after me, or Henry, or someone else to lash out at me.

Miles opened the back door, helped me in, and closed the door behind me.

He slipped into the front seat and laid his arm over the back of the bench seat.

Then, to my immense surprise, he smiled at me.

"Where did you ever learn to act like that?" he asked.

I stared at him. Had he not heard what I'd said to Jocelyn? How stupidly I had revealed our purpose? "What do you mean?"

"With Henry," he said, his grin growing. "It was as if you were an entirely different woman, the way you flirted with him."

"Joan fancies herself an actress and dreams of being in motion pictures someday," I said. "When we were younger, she always had me run lines with her."

He nodded appreciatively. "Impressive," he said.

It wasn't especially. For all he knew, that could have simply been natural behavior for me. It was not as if he really knew me. Still, it was good to be told I had pulled something off well. I was still smarting over having forgotten my mission with Jocelyn.

With great relief, I heard the car engine start up.

"I realized you were saying more than you intended back there, so I thought it best to get us both away in a hurry," Miles said. "But it's quite simple what happened; your emotions, most specifically your grief over the death of your uncle, got the better of you."

I stared at the back of his head, as the car pulled away from the curb. I couldn't exactly deny it, could I?

"She knew immediately what I was thinking," I said. "Even before I accused her, I think Jocelyn knew right away that I suspected her of killing Uncle Walter."

Miles said nothing for a moment as he took a right turn, away from the jazz club.

"It strikes me that she was more distressed than I had expected," I said. "Though I don't know her well enough to say whether her reaction was real or feigned."

Still he said nothing.

I gazed out the window and sighed heavily. "And so, we are no closer to finding out who killed him," I said. "I learned nothing from Henry, and Jocelyn neither admitted nor denied anything." I groaned, shaking my head. "If I hadn't allowed my feelings to get in the way, then maybe we would have gotten somewhere..."

"Well, we did learn something," Miles said. "She and the bartender clearly had some sort of relationship. Whether it is ongoing or in the past, there is still at least some affection from him toward her."

"And her toward him," I said. "When she told me he wouldn't be good for me, I don't think she was just trying to look out for my interests. What reason would she have for doing that now? Since she and Uncle Walter didn't marry, it isn't as if we are family."

"True," he said, sparing me a quick glance over his shoulder.

"What if she had planned to just take his money and run?" I asked. "Run off with Henry so they could live happily?"

"It isn't a bad idea...but wouldn't she have to wait to kill your uncle until after they were married?" Miles asked. "Otherwise, she would inherit nothing but whatever trinkets he may have already given her."

I hesitated, thinking through his words. "I don't know," I said. "But her anger, her desire to move the wedding up – "

"May have been nothing more than that," Miles said. "It's entirely possible that she wished to marry him for his money, *and* that she had nothing to do with his death. She could be entirely innocent in that regard."

I frowned. It troubled me that she could have been so mercenary, but he was right that she might have had nothing to do with the death. One did not equate to the other.

"It would be poor planning to kill him before the wedding," he went on. "If she had any sense, she would have wanted to make sure she had all her things in order, that he had signed over his entire fortune, before doing anything drastic. If she is as calculating as you think her, would she have made such a clumsy move?"

He slowed the car as another car had stopped up ahead to let a passenger out, and looked back at me. "Really think about it for a moment. She would probably have needed this Henry fellow to assist her, if she was going to push your uncle to his death. And if the two of them schemed together, would they have ruined their own plan by acting prematurely?"

"Perhaps plans went awry?" I suggested halfheartedly. "Or perhaps there was an argument and everyone's emotions ran away with them, overruling the plan?"

But then, I relented. "You may be right. Perhaps it doesn't make sense..."

He nodded, turning around. "I suggest, for the time being, we forget this Jocelyn. Unless we find any incriminating evidence, of course. Then, we would be wise to revisit the idea."

I murmured agreement, gazing out the window again.

He said nothing further as he drove me back to Sutton Place, for which I was grateful, because I needed the silence to think.

9

M y encounter with Jocelyn was discouraging.

All I can hope is that my father will come to his senses and take control of the situation, I thought that night as I locked myself in my room with nothing more than Mrs. Riley's cocoa for company. *I never should have thought I could do anything about it in the first place. I am no expert on such things. I should be leaving this to the police.*

I glanced at the drawer of my writing desk where I'd hidden the letter I found in my uncle's room. If the police came looking, I would give it to them. With a bit of luck, I might receive nothing more than stern looks and a threatening lecture for taking something from that hotel room. My family's status would probably protect me from any harsher penalty for tampering with a possible crime scene.

I hoped more than anything that life could return to some sort of normalcy. I hoped the current financial dilemma would right itself as such things always seemed to do, and that my father's indifferent attitude toward his brother's death could dissipate when he was no longer quite so distracted. I did my best to give him the benefit of the doubt, knowing he was under a great deal of stress.

Perhaps all I could do for now was to wait...

THREE DAYS LATER, nothing much had changed.

I sat in the drawing room with my mother and Joan, trying my best to finish the chapter of a book. I had read it three times before, but as it was a favorite of mine since childhood, I often found myself drawn to it in times of distress. Unfortunately for me, though, my mind seemed intent on dwelling on all the things it shouldn't, and as such, I could not focus to read even one line.

I snapped the book shut, looking across the room at my mother. "Mother?" I asked. "Are we not to have a funeral for Uncle Walter?"

She looked up from the game of checkers she was playing with Joan, and stared blankly at me. "Darling, I thought your father told you not to bring any of this up again," she said.

"Today should have been the day we would be attending," I said. "Traditionally."

"Yes, well, these are unconventional times," Mother said vaguely. "Your father has many urgent matters to concern himself with."

"More urgent than – " I began, and then cut myself off. Giving way to my frustration would accomplish nothing. I thought of Jocelyn, and tried to gather myself. "Mother, has he said nothing about it? Nothing at all?"

Joan turned in her chair and regarded me with a raised eyebrow. "Sylvia, I don't believe this is the time."

I held my following words. It wasn't unlike Joan to contradict me, but in front of Mother we almost always agreed. I looked down at my hand lying across the book cover. My fingers curled up underneath my palm, making a tense fist.

The door opened and Miles strode in. "Good afternoon, ma'am," he said to Mother. "And good afternoon to you as well, Miss Joan and Miss Sylvia."

I didn't look up at him, but made sure to nevertheless force a quick, tight smile onto my face. I opened the book to an inconsequential page and tried to make it appear as if I were reading.

"My word. Miles, how is it that you are always so

chipper?" Mother asked. "And I have said it once and I'll say it again; I just love that accent."

Miles stopped beside the fireplace, kneeling to draw a few logs from the pile nestled beside the fire. He tossed the logs into the hearth. "Well, madam, I am always grateful for my position in your house and try to show it. I find it a great honor to be here."

Mother chuckled happily. "My friends will all be so envious when I tell them I have found a proper English butler for my home. I am so tickled that Mrs. Riley brought you on when she did, Miles. It could not have been timelier."

Out of the corner of my eye, I noticed Jo turn just enough to shoot me a glance. I still had yet to tell her that I had been the one to find Miles.

"I call it destiny, Mrs. Shipman," Miles said politely.

Mother giggled again but did not have the chance to respond.

"There you are," came our father's voice. I hadn't heard him come into the room.

"Oh, darling, do come in," Mother said. "For once, I am winning at checkers."

"Very nice, my dear," Father said.

I watched as he strode up to the back of the sofa but no further. His gaze hardened and I noticed even deeper circles beneath his eyes. His attention fell on me and then on Joan.

"I need one of you girls to make a trip down to Walter's house," he said.

I stared at him. The tone he used sounded as if nothing had happened, as if Uncle Walter was still alive. "Uncle Walter's?" I asked, my voice unsteady.

"What for?" Joan asked, clearly thinking the same thing that I was.

"I need you to pick up a few things of mine that apparently have been set aside for me," Father said with a sniff, pulling the lapel of his jacket closed and fastening the top button.

I could only stare at him in disbelief. He dared not mention his brother in the past three days but evidently now felt enough time had passed that it was acceptable to speak of him. How did this make any sense?

The answer was obvious; it didn't make sense.

"Well, *I* certainly cannot go," Joan said, folding her arms. "I have the luncheon for Maryanne today. She is to be married tomorrow, remember?"

My insides went cold at the thought of entering Uncle Walter's house alone. I was not superstitious but my secret visit to my uncle's hotel room had been quite unnerving enough for me. It was never pleasant to return to a place recently used by someone who had died.

I turned my gaze on her. "Joan, we could go together," I said, my hand reaching for the small, silver key at my throat. "I am certain it would not take long and you could be back before – "

"It's on the other side of the city," Joan said, which I knew perfectly well to be true. "It will take us an hour to get there, at the very least. No, I'm sorry, Father, but I cannot go."

"Leave her be, Cecil," Mother said, not bothering to lift her eyes from the game board. "If she is busy, then she is busy. Send Sylvia. I'm certain she has nothing better to do today."

I stared at her next, feeling helpless. *Mother, why would you send me? Me, of all people?*

She smiled, apparently oblivious to my internal struggle. "It will be nice for you, dear. When was the last time you got out of this house?"

Three days ago, when I went to that jazz club, I thought immediately. I hadn't wanted to go out since. The mood of the entire city seemed dark and depressing lately. It was much easier to carry on as normal from the comforts of my own home.

"Mother, would you care to accompany me, then?" I asked. "I do not recall if you've had the chance for an outing recently."

Mother shook her head, her mahogany curls swinging. "No, dear. I have little desire to step into Walter's home at the moment. The thought is much too gloomy. Besides, I am waiting on some friends to arrive. It's our weekly game day, don't forget."

I wanted to ask why my father wasn't going himself, but the question simply would not rise to my lips as he stared at me, his mouth downturned and his gaze as hard as stone.

"You'll have a nice time, dear," Mother said. "Getting all that fresh air for yourself."

I looked around. Joan seemed to be the only one who held any sympathy for me, which she demonstrated with a small shrug of one shoulder.

"I...I suppose I shall go get ready, then," I said, slowly rising from the chair. I gingerly set my book down and crossed the room.

I stopped as I drew near my father.

"What am I to be looking for?" I asked.

"I'm not exactly sure, as I wasn't informed of the details. I imagine the servants will have set it aside somewhere," he said. "Some books, likely. Perhaps something that belonged to our father. Not much."

I nodded and withdrew from the drawing room.

I started down the hall, anxious knots twisting and writhing in my stomach like a pile of provoked snakes. I had been involved enough in the death of my uncle. I had thought it was time to step back from the whole matter, and yet, fate seemed to be sending me a different message.

"I presume you will be needing my services, Miss Sylvia?"

I stopped to look over my shoulder, finding Miles

hovering near the wall. He studied me, his brows lifted, his green eyes alert.

"Yes, I suppose I will," I said. "I only need to fetch my coat and hat. I shall be down in just a moment."

I rushed up the stairs, wondering how much of my family's conversation he had overheard. And why should it make me uncomfortable if he heard all? It was perfectly normal for a butler to know the goings on of the family he served. It was not as if there was anything furtive or calculating in his hovering about, always listening in the background. It was his duty, after all, to be on hand at all times in case we had need of him.

I shook my head. I was simply becoming paranoid about these things. I must trust the man or I wouldn't have hired him.

And I did trust him, I remembered, though I could not explain why. Ever since I had met him in that alleyway near the hotel, I had been prepared to take a risk with him and he had seemingly returned the favor all along.

Just look at what happened with Jocelyn, I thought. My family knew nothing of the incident and I intended it to remain that way. Miles had not yet said anything, nor did I think he would. For some reason, a reason I couldn't quite place, I really believed he would not betray me.

I snatched a thick wool coat from my wardrobe and

fussed over a pair of hats to wear. In the end, I chose the green one...and *not* because it's earthy richness reminded me of a certain butler's eyes.

Miles opened the car door for me and said nothing until we had pulled away from Sutton Place.

"It may not be my place to say, Miss, but I believe your father is asking unfairly for you to take on a task that he himself should be doing," Miles said as we took a familiar left turn past the corner post office where I sent letters to friends and cards to my grandmother in upstate.

"You're right that you shouldn't say so," I said. "But I have to confess I have the same opinion, as well."

It was comforting to know someone had sympathy for my situation, even if it wasn't of much practical use. We may have both been correct but that didn't change the fact that I was still sitting in the car, on the way to my uncle's, and my father was still at home.

"In truth, it seems as if he is frightened of facing the facts about his brother's death," Miles said with a brief glance at me in the rearview mirror. "I think he is so troubled by it that he simply cannot bear setting foot in that house."

"Then why does he think Joan or I would be better equipped?" I asked. "What makes him think it would be any easier for us?"

"I wonder if he is unable to see past the end of his nose in this matter," Miles said. "He is so consumed with his own worry and troubles maybe he has not stopped to think how this is affecting the rest of his family."

"That is being very gracious," I said, with perhaps more acid than I intended.

Miles shrugged. "Nevertheless...I think this was a shortsighted plan and he should never have asked you to do it."

I didn't answer but my insides felt as cold as the chill from the window beside me. *He thinks my father is a coward,* I thought. *Is he right?*

"Which is why..." Miles began as we slowed to a halt at a traffic stop. An officer was standing out in the middle of the intersection with his whistle, guiding the traffic around. Miles turned to look at me. "I would be perfectly willing to go in and find whatever it is that needs to be found. If you like, you could stay here and wait in the car. There is no reason you need to subject yourself to this."

I shook my head. "It's all right," I said. "I'll be fine. Besides, you wouldn't know where to look."

"I'm certain someone will be able to guide me," he said. "It wouldn't be entirely unusual for a servant to run such an errand. No one will think anything of it, I'm sure."

I paused, considering. Maybe that would be the best idea. My father would never have to know I didn't actually set foot in the house myself, nor would he care. He would still be receiving the items he was looking for. If Miles was willing to do this for me, why should I stop him?

When we arrived at my uncle's, sadness stirred in me as I stared up at the house. No more would we enjoy our yearly Christmas dinner there. No more would we stand on those front steps to watch the Independence Day parades. No more would we catch glimpses of the sunset over the water from the top floor, from the round window of that tiny study on the southwestern side of the house.

I sat back in my seat, unable to keep staring at the red brick house.

"I shall not be long," Miles said. "Here, perhaps a novel to entertain you in my absence?" He presented me with a book, the corners worn and the pages yellowing.

I took it, turning it over. The back cover looked as if it had been patched in the bottom right corner.

"That should keep you busy," Miles said with a flash of a grin. He closed the door and was off.

I flipped open the front page and noticed a handwritten note on the front cover.

To Nicholas, with all my love.

Nicholas? Who was Nicholas?

There was a series of taps on the window. I glanced up to see Miles looking down at me.

I pushed open the door and he pulled it open the

rest of the way. "I'm terribly sorry, Miss Sylvia, but I may need your help after all."

"What's the matter?" I asked.

"Well...it might be better if I could show you," he said.

"Of course," I said, climbing out. "What happened?"

"It's the strangest thing," he said as we started toward the steps together. "There is a note affixed to the door. I don't believe anyone is here."

"No one?" I asked, bewildered.

I saw the note before I could make out what it said. I hurried to it and frowned at its short explanation. *Estate sale, coming this Wednesday. Ten to four.*

An estate sale but no funeral? This entire business just kept growing stranger.

I knocked on the door and waited, listening. There was no immediate response. I grabbed hold of the knocker on the front of the door and gave it a few more good raps. Still, nothing.

"How odd," I said, frowning at the door. "Why isn't anyone answering?"

"I don't know," Miles said. "I tried the door and, not surprisingly, it's locked."

I did the same, trying hard more than a few times to really twist the knob. Nothing happened.

I stepped back and looked up at the windows.

Drapes were drawn shut and I could find no light in the windows. How strange.

"Why would someone contact my father and ask him to fetch his things if there would be no one here to receive him?" I asked aloud.

"That is my thought as well," Miles said. "Unless the message your father received was some days old."

I tried to peer in through the window beside the door, and frowned. "His furniture is just as it always is," I said. "It doesn't seem as if anything is out of place."

"Could they have relocated all his staff already?" Miles asked.

"I have no idea..." I said. "And who would have?"

It troubled me to think someone was taking charge of my uncle's home and things in this hasty way. Surely it wasn't his adult children yet, when they had not even traveled to town since his death?

"I am beginning to wonder if the person who killed your uncle has had any say in what has happened since his death," Miles said.

"What are you saying?" I asked.

He nodded up at the house. "I'm saying it's appearing more and more likely that whoever killed him was someone quite close to him," he said. "It seems very unusual that his house would be turned over so quickly, even amidst the uncertain financial climate at the moment."

I frowned. "I have trouble believing Jocelyn would

be capable of this," I said. "She wouldn't have the legal authority anyway."

Miles looked at me. "No, she doesn't strike me as the sort who would have the connections to sidestep the usual procedures. Whoever is doing this is sure to have a great deal of control over your uncle's life, in some way or form."

I looked around. "My father will be most displeased if I return home without those items," I said.

"You can't help that no one is here," Miles said. "Surely he wouldn't be angry with you over that."

"You don't know my father very well," I said. "He will get something in his mind and be unable to shake it. If I return home empty-handed, he will not hear my reasons why. He will simply scold me and send me back out."

I turned and headed down the stairs again, making my way to the side of the townhome. Running between my uncle's home and the house to his left was a narrow alley, hardly wide enough for a man to slip through. "I do, however, also know my uncle," I said. "And I know there is likely a way to get in that no one thought to check."

"Oh?" Miles asked, following after me.

I stared at the gap and steadied my shaking hands by balling them into fists.

"Miss Sylvia?" Miles asked, drawing up beside me. "Are you all right?"

"What? Oh, yes. I'm fine," I said, not looking at him, instead staring down the incredibly long path, wondering just how I was going to fit through there. The walls seemingly leaned in toward one another like the beak of some great creature.

"Are you quite sure?" he asked. "You seem suddenly pale."

I licked my lips but my mouth had gone dry.

"Is it the narrow space?" he asked. "Because that's understandable enough. It's not all that uncommon to be frightened of tight places."

I sniffed, the cold making my nose start to drip. "I have never gone through to the back of his house in this way. I've never had to go down there."

"Here, take my hand," he said. "I shall lead you through. You can close your eyes, if you like."

I stared blankly at him for a moment, but it was certainly better than the alternative. "All right," I said. "I just – "

"I'll take care to make sure you don't trip over anything," he said. "Don't worry about that."

"Very well," I said, holding my hand out.

He took it in his own. "Whenever you are ready, you can close your eyes."

I did. My throat became tight and I held my breath

as the light pressing against my eyelids faded to darkness. We were in the narrow way.

I counted my heartbeats as we walked and tried to listen to the calming sound of our footsteps. Miles moved slowly and deliberately, saying reassuring things to me as we went. I didn't hear a word he said, as all I could think about was how close the walls were on either side of me. Drawing my shoulders in, I imagined the scrape of the bricks against the shoulders of my coat, somehow scratching through to my skin –

"We've made it," Miles said a moment later.

My eyes flew open and I looked around. He was right. We were standing out in the much wider alleyway behind my uncle's house. It was over.

"Thank you," I said, already feeling my breathing return to normal. "That was...better than I had expected."

He nodded and turned to look up at my uncle's house. "Now, what was your idea to get in?" he asked.

Thankful for the opportunity to distract myself, I made my way to the stone steps leading down to the ground floor where the back door to the kitchen was tucked away. I tried the door and smiled when it opened easily.

"It's unlocked," I said, hoping no one else in the vicinity heard me. Miles came swiftly down the stairs after me and we made our way inside.

I went in to the kitchen and it struck me just how

quiet it all was. I had not been there many times, but when I had, the heat from the large stove had warmed the room. There had been the bustle of servants, the boiling of pots, the diligent chopping of vegetables and seasoned meats. Now, the space stood empty, dark, and cold.

I had recently seen my uncle, lying dead in the middle of that hotel foyer...and yet, somehow the empty kitchen troubled me more deeply than the surreal sight of him ever could have. It displayed how despite the knowledge I had, he really was never, ever coming back. There was no changing it. His story, his place in my life, was now in the past.

I lingered there for only a moment, giving myself a chance to brush against the sadness, then I strode out into the dark hallway beyond.

I did not allow myself the luxury of spending time in any of the other rooms I had frequented throughout my childhood years. I didn't give myself a moment to look at the fireplace where Joan and I would sit and read together on cold, winter nights while Father talked business with Uncle Walter. I passed right by the dining room where they had surprised me with a lavish dinner party for my sixteenth birthday, where all my friends had been invited...including a certain Mr. Lawson. I ignored the closet near the front door where I'd hid, time and again, when Joan and I would play hide and seek with our older cousins; they always seemed to forget that the long coats inside made the perfect curtain for the game.

I could not ignore the differences, though. Books had been stacked in odd piles up and down the main hall, along with a number of other loose items like a lamp, a tea set, and a gilded bird cage that had once belonged to my aunt.

"This is strange…" I said, gesturing to one such pile inside the door to my uncle's personal study. "I wonder if my cousins have been here after all, to arrange these things."

"I wonder if they are part of your cousins' inheritance?" Miles asked. "I imagine in the event of his death, all of his assets will be given to them."

I nodded. I had not the heart to write to any of them, uncertain what I could possibly say. Anytime I had thought of it, everything I could come up with sounded hollow and disingenuous.

"I imagine Father's things will be in here somewhere," I said, looking around at the mess that my uncle's study always was. Despite the usual clutter, I could see that even this room had been organized into additional piles, mostly of books and journals. "I will likely recognize them if I see them."

"It seems there are notes attached to the stacks," Miles said, turning over a torn piece of paper that had been tied to a series of books all bound in the same blue leather. "Your father's things might be labeled, as well."

"That's good to know," I said. I started to examine the stacks, finding some names I was familiar with, others I wasn't. It was thorough, that was for sure. How had someone already had time to do all this? It must have taken hours.

Thankfully, it didn't take long to find what I sought. Sitting in the leather desk chair, someone had left a collection of books, pens, and even a box filled with my father's favorite sealing wax. It had the family insignia engraved on the small stamp inside, with a large S. I hoisted the stack into my arms, surprised that it was not bigger. I turned to find Miles, to see if he might carry some of it back outside. "Miles?" I asked. "Miles, where are you?"

"Over here," he said, around the side of one of the book cases. In the corner, my uncle had deemed the portion of the wall between the window and the fireplace an odd space, and so had created a sort of alcove with a few shelves.

I wandered over there and found Miles peering intently at the back shelf.

"This is where he kept his most treasured tomes, in the hope of shielding them from burglars, should any break in," I explained.

Miles didn't seem to hear me and instead reached for a copy at the very end of the row. I might have missed it, as it was almost the same color as the cherry stained wood beside it and tucked all the way toward the back beside a gaudy green and gold gilded tome.

"Why does your uncle have a copy of this?" he asked.

I stared at the unassuming book in his hands. It was thin and plain, with a simple title in black script. "I have never seen that before," I said, taking a step closer. "What is it?"

Miles moved it away, passing it to his other hand, out of my reach. "This is a manual of sorts..." he said, his brow furrowing.

"You look as if it might come to life and take your hand off," I said, curiosity growing inside me.

He hesitated. "Rumor has it this book's author was once associated with a group of criminals here in town, a connection that eventually cost him his life," he said.

I frowned. "You mean gangsters? Where did you hear of such a thing?"

"I'm surprised you haven't. The author is rather infamous, I believe," he said. "What's less well known is that his works have become rare, and that those most likely to collect them are his old associates."

I paled. "What exactly are you implying about my uncle?"

Miles shrugged. "I am not implying anything. It's possible your uncle simply took an interest in rare books. However...I do not believe anyone would be able to get their hands on a copy of this one unless it was given to them personally."

A chill swept through me and it had nothing to do with the bitter draft in the large, empty house. Still, I found it difficult to accept his words. "You seem to know a great deal about such an unusual subject," I said, my voice slightly accusatory.

He shrugged. "I've had some...unusual friends on the streets. Not criminals, mind you, but people with access to information. And they liked to talk about their pasts, probably more than was wise."

"Well, I cannot believe Uncle Walter would have any sort of criminal associations," I said.

"You do not have to believe it," Miles said. "But you do have to realize your uncle died in a very suspicious manner. If he had any unsavory connections, it might explain a great deal."

I drew my brows together. "I know – I *knew* my uncle. He was an honest man."

Miles nodded. "And he very well may not have had anything to do with them," he said. "But we must be open to the possibility."

I tried to swallow but it was as if a stone had lodged itself in my throat. "What is inside?" I asked, gesturing to the book.

"I don't know," Miles said. "I have only heard of it. I have no idea what it says."

"Maybe we should look," I said. "Maybe it's not the book you are thinking of."

Miles gave me a brief, disbelieving look before flipping open the front cover.

A note lay inside, on a separate sheet of paper. Age had almost sealed it to the page.

"What does it say?" I asked.

Miles lifted the book up closer to his nose. "It's difficult to read," he said. "But I believe it says, *Use wisely. Once you begin down this path, you can never turn around.*"

He handed the book to me.

"So you can see that I am not making it up," he said plainly.

I took it, and despite the small size, it felt heavier than any thousand page tome I had ever held. I read the words on the page and found he had been correct.

I handed it back. "I still do not know if this book has anything to do with his death," I said.

Miles frowned, pocketing the book. "I am sorry, Miss Sylvia, but I have to disagree..." he said. "Ties like these would most *certainly* have something to do with his death, if he got mixed up with such people."

10

"Somehow I have two bits of evidence and yet no clue who they could be tied to," I said as Miles pulled the car up outside my family's home in Sutton Place. "If anything, this whole affair went from bad to worse."

"Unfortunately, that is how things often work," Miles said as he turned the ignition off. He had been quiet, to allow me the chance to think all the way home. Finding the book had certainly caught me off guard, but more than that, had made me begin to question a great deal about the people I knew...and what secrets they might have.

"How do you handle these matters so casually?" I asked him. "Nothing ever seems to surprise or distress you."

Miles glanced briefly at me in the rearview mirror.

"I have seen a great many things over the course of my life," he said. "One becomes accustomed to the unexpected."

He did not elaborate any further as he exited the vehicle and came around to let me out.

We climbed the front steps to the house and he opened the door, allowing me to pass through ahead of him. "I shall go and fetch your father's things from the car," he said, and started back down the steps.

Inside, I removed the scarf from my neck and hung it on the rack near the door.

"There you are!"

Joan glared at me from the top of the stairs, her hands on her hips.

I blinked up at her. "What's the matter?" I asked. "Did something – "

"Nothing happened," she said, huffing as she came down, taking a deliberately long time on each stair. "Well, nothing more than the usual. Father is in a tizzy, Mother is in her own world..." She shook her head. "What took you so long at Uncle Walter's house?"

"We had trouble getting inside," I said.

Jo frowned at me, her eyes narrowing. "Why?"

I looked over her shoulder, up the stairs. "They seem to be getting it ready for an estate sale next week," I said.

"You aren't lying..." Jo said, her gaze sharpening

further. "But you aren't telling me the whole truth, either…"

Before she could ask any more questions, Miles came in. "Good afternoon, Miss Joan," he said, his arms laden with Father's things. He pushed the door closed behind him with his heel. "I take it all has been well in our absence?"

"You'll have to ask Father yourself," she said, folding her arms. "He's in his study. He will likely want to see you and all the items you've brought."

"Certainly," Miles said, inclining his head as he started for the stairs. "I will be happy to oblige."

I watched him walk away, feeling both relieved and somewhat anxious.

"You and I need to have a talk," Joan said sternly.

Before I could protest, she steered me up the stairs and down the hall to her room.

She thrust me down onto the bench at the foot of her bed, standing over me with her arms still firmly crossed and her dark blue eyes flashing.

"What's this about?" I asked, but the red in my cheeks revealed that I knew perfectly well why I was there.

"Ever since the night Uncle Walter died, you have been acting strangely," Joan said. "You are obviously keeping some sort of secret and I want to know what it is."

"Joan..." I said. "You must know that I am not trying to keep anything from you, it's just – "

"You have never held onto a secret for this long," she said, her eyes narrowing further. "Not in our entire lives."

"This is different," I said. "There's so much I don't know, and until I do, it seems best to keep things quiet – "

"Does it have to do with me?" she asked, her brows leaping toward her hairline, disappearing beneath her wispy bangs.

"No, not at all," I said.

"Then what is it?" she asked. "Maybe I can help, whatever it is!"

"I don't know..." I said.

I stared up at her, and she looked down at me in a way that she hadn't done since she was twelve or thirteen years old; she stuck her bottom lip out and gave me her best doe eyes.

"Fine!" I relented, getting to my feet. "Fine, I will tell you, but this must stay between us. You cannot go down and blab to Mother or to any of your friends. All right?"

"Yes, all right, all right," she said with a few fervent nods. "It will not leave this room."

"Very well," I said. I drew in a deep breath to try and calm my nerves. "I believe Uncle Walter was murdered."

Her eyes widened and her mouth dropped open. "What?" Slowly, she sank down onto the bench where I had been sitting, her gaze distant. "But...how?" she asked. Her vision focused again and she looked up at me. "How do you know?"

I gave her a quick explanation of everything I had seen and heard up to that point. I told her about sneaking into the hotel room and about the note I'd found. I told her what I had learned at the jazz club and about my fight with Jocelyn. I told her about what I had seen at Uncle Walter's. I held nothing back, apart from the fact that Miles had been assisting me so much. It seemed best not to drag him into the story.

She sat and listened, saying nothing until I was finished. She simply stared at me, her expression becoming more and more astonished as I went on.

"Sylvia, this – this is madness," she said as I finished my tale. "You need to get yourself out of this. It's too dangerous."

"I know," I admitted. "I tried to get out of it, but then Father sent me off to his house, and Miles recognized that book – "

"How do you know Miles even knew what he was talking about?" Joan asked, crossing her arms. "He's our butler, for heaven's sake, and seems a very imaginative one, at that."

"I don't know..." I said. "He acted very concerned about it."

"And how did he know what it was in the first place?" she asked, echoing my own thoughts. "That seems like very specific knowledge."

"I thought the same," I said. "But he says he has known a great many people and heard many stories. I..." I hesitated. "I don't think he wanted to discuss his past. It must be too personal."

Joan's exasperated expression deepened. "Wonderful. We have a servant with a secret personal life, and you are too polite to pry into *his* business, although you don't mind exploring everyone else's. And speaking of you...why are you so determined to hold onto this matter with Uncle Walter? Why do you wish to put yourself into situations that could be dangerous?"

"I don't – " I said. "I am not trying to do anything of the sort."

"Yet you are," she said. "Do you not realize just how bad this looks for you? I'm not the only one to have noticed how bizarrely you have been acting. Mrs. Riley, for one, made mention of it just this morning."

"Did she?" I asked. I had not thought I was being so obvious.

"Yes," Joan said. "And that's to say nothing of what Mother thinks."

"What do you mean? What has she said?" I asked.

"She thinks you are out with some man," Joan said.

"Someone you haven't shared about with the rest of the family."

I sank back down onto the bench beside her. "Oh dear..." I said, eyeing her.

"Oh dear, indeed," Joan said. "She is simply delighted. I think she is hoping you are going to announce an engagement, or something close to it, any day now."

I sighed. "This is a mess."

"Yes, it is," Joan said. "You must straighten it out, Sylvia, before things get any worse. We do not need any more troubles in this family. Father has enough on his mind."

"I know, I know," I muttered.

"You have attracted enough negative attention around town lately anyway," she went on. "Especially after the fallout with Mr. Lawson – " She quickly stopped. "I'm sorry. I know he was positively terrible. I should not have mentioned him at all."

I refused to be drawn into that particular subject. "This whole ordeal isn't worth it," I admitted. "I am grieved over what happened to Uncle Walter but you are right. It isn't my duty to look into it. I never should have allowed myself to get wrapped up in the matter."

...But what about the man fleeing down the fire escape? a small voice at the back of my mind questioned. *No one else will act on that information if I don't...*

"And what about this strange relationship you

seem to have with our new servant?" Joan asked, turning back on me. "You still haven't told me how he came to work at our house and how you seem to know so much about it."

I hesitated. I hadn't told her I had found Miles down the alleyway that night, only that I'd seen the man running away. I hadn't told her I had chased him, knowing how foolish it would make me sound. For that matter, it might not reflect well on Miles either.

"I met Miles the night of the dinner, at the hotel," I said. "He impressed me with his skills and so I suggested that he come here. I was sure Mrs. Riley would know whether or not he would be up to snuff."

It was a carefully worded explanation that could be interrupted however the hearer chose.

"He has been extraordinarily helpful, I will admit to that," Joan said, shifting her gaze to her bedroom door. "Father likes his driving, and I have never known a butler to so accurately anticipate the needs of those around him. He knew Mother wanted her book and pillow before her afternoon nap in the parlor, even before she had told him. He brought hot chamomile tea to help her sleep, and I do not believe I heard her stir for over an hour."

"I'm glad to hear he is settling in well," I said. "Especially glad that Father is pleased."

"As pleased as he can be about anything lately..." she said, crossing her arms.

"Has anything changed?" I asked. "About the money problems? I haven't had the heart to ask."

Joan sighed. "I don't know," she said. "He is being eerily quiet about the whole thing."

"Which is worrying in and of itself," I muttered.

Joan frowned at the door. "He will likely want to ask what you learned at Uncle Walter's. You should go speak to him."

"Right…" I said, getting to my feet.

I made my way to my father's study, my mind racing. Joan was right. It was high time that I leave behind my questions about my uncle's death. It didn't matter that I knew what I did. I could hand it over to my father, say I found it all at Uncle Walter's house, and allow him to deal with it…or choose to leave it alone.

Miles had continually asked if I wanted to drop the matter and I had just allowed myself to get swept up in it. I should have said "no!" from the very beginning, and stood firm, regardless of what happened around me. I loved my uncle, of course, but that didn't mean I had to be the one to avenge him. I could, and should, leave it to someone else to do.

I rounded the corner near Father's study, still uncertain.

"Cecil, we cannot, and I do mean *cannot* have anyone thinking this has any tie to us – to you." The voice, hushed yet fervent, belonged to Frank Morrow.

"Don't you think I realize that?" my father answered, equally sharply. "It's what I thought the moment he was pronounced dead."

I blanched, nearly tripping over the edge of the rug. I stumbled and managed to catch myself on the wall, but only just. My heart thumped wildly in my chest and my insides went cold. *Pronounced dead?* I thought, wondering if I was going mad. *And what do they mean, cannot have anyone tying this to them?*

"Those were his...friends," Mr. Morrow continued. "Not yours. We have to make that perfectly plain."

"If I say a word, it will draw suspicion regardless," Father spat in return. "It is best if I do nothing."

"But if you were to dismiss those suspicions – " Mr. Morrow began.

" – They will have them all the same," Father hissed. "It matters not what I say. Thus far, saying nothing, *doing* nothing, has garnered success."

"Thus far," Mr. Morrow repeated. "But there have been rumblings, Cecil. People wondering – "

"Let them wonder," Father said. "I need not admit to anything."

I hesitated, glancing up and down the hall. No one else was around. I wondered if Miles was in the room with them but I highly doubted Father would be so vocal around a new employee.

"I agree with you, of course," Mr. Morrow said. "I

just thought it best that you know people have been talking."

I heard a *smack* of something against the desk, perhaps a book or something else equally heavy. "Then what am I to do, Frank?" Father asked. "Given what's happened..."

"You and I, we have had nothing to do with it," Mr. Morrow said. "This is far bigger than a tip off that just happened to come to pass."

A tip off? I wondered, my mind racing. *Surely they cannot mean the same hint that Uncle Walter's letter spoke of?*

"It all is connected..." Father said. "I am not dimwitted enough to think otherwise."

"No one has suggested you are," Mr. Morrow said.

Father remained quiet for a moment.

I knew I should turn and go. This conversation had nothing to do with me.

But it does have to do with Uncle Walter. And with what I know.

"I cannot afford to have any of Walter's connections coming back to haunt me," my father said. "I have lost too much as it is."

Did Father already see the letter, before I found it? I pondered. *I know it wasn't written by Uncle Walter...but did Father not recognize that? Does he somehow think the letter was genuine?*

Or, perhaps he hadn't read the letter, but what if

Uncle Walter spoke to him in confidence before his death? It was entirely possible the contents of the letter were true, but it was simply not penned by him.

I rubbed my temples. This was all so terribly confusing.

Something happened that night in my uncle's room that I know nothing about, I realized. *A conversation, a visit, or a threat... Something occurred that led to all of this. And my father knows a great deal more than he is letting on.*

"I hope you know I will do everything I can for you, just as I did for your brother," Mr. Morrow went on. "I have known you both for a long, long time. We may not always have seen eye to eye, and I might have questioned your financial decisions once or twice, but you must know I have always seen you and Walter as my friends, first and foremost."

A heavy sigh followed his words, along with the *clink* of something, maybe a coffee cup, being set down on a hard surface.

"I did wonder..." Mr. Morrow said, a bit hesitantly. "What was it you and he spoke about that night when you went up to his room?"

Father remained silent but I sensed his tension. "So, now you are turning the blame on *me*," he said in a low, grumbling tone. "I wondered if you might."

Mr. Morrow said nothing.

My mouth went dry, my stomach dropping to the floor. Mr. Morrow was accusing my father? What was he talking about? What conversation had my father privately had with my uncle?

"Be on your way, Frank," Father said, ice coating his words. "I have a great deal that must get done by tomorrow. I shall see you on Friday."

As Mr. Morrow murmured agreement and prepared to depart, I suddenly realized I was standing in a very visible place.

11

Footsteps sounded on the other side of the door, and fear pulsed through me. I was sure to be caught just out in the hall. And if they found me out here, they would know I had heard most of what they had been saying.

I needed to look as if I was here for some innocent purpose. I had come to see my father, yes, and this was my house, yes...but it would be horrendously suspicious if I stood as I was just outside the door, waiting.

I looked wildly around. I couldn't duck into one of the rooms at the end of the hall in time, and I didn't think I could make it appear believable that I had only just arrived.

Instead, just as the door to the study swung open, I plopped myself down across the hall in one of the chairs that was more for decorative purpose than for everyday use. I reached for a small vase of dried flowers and settled them in my lap just as Mr. Morrow strode from the study, bidding my father goodbye with a nod of his head.

I hoped the anxiousness was not as clear on my face as I felt it was.

He noticed me as he turned to start up the hall, and stopped, shaking his head. "Sylvia..." he said, and I noticed the smile on his face did not reach his eyes. "Good afternoon."

I grinned up at him, trying to breathe deeply through my nose to quiet my rapid heart. "Hello, Mr. Morrow," I said. "Here to see my father, too?"

"Yes..." he said, turning to give the study door a hard look. "I'm sorry if we kept you waiting."

"Oh, no, it's all right," I said. "I only waited a moment or two. I was up in Joan's room."

Mr. Morrow nodded, looking behind him once more. "Mhmm," he mumbled. "How have you been doing? Since Walter's passing, that is."

"Oh..." I said, and I couldn't stop my face from falling. "It's been difficult on us. Perhaps on Father most of all."

"I think you are right about that," he said, almost under his breath. His brow wrinkled, the glass lenses in his round spectacles glinting. "I can understand if it would distress you to answer," he said. "But are you aware of what your father and uncle talked about the night he died?"

A cold chill swept through me, as I stared up at him. It was quickly becoming clear that whatever my father had said to my uncle was deeply concerning. What was even stranger was that my father refused to share the subject of their discussion with Mr. Morrow. He usually told him more than I believed he ever shared with my mother. Frank Morrow was his most trusted financial advisor, as well as his close friend.

So why is he not telling anyone what was said that night? I wondered.

"I...have no idea," I said, shaking my head help-lessly. "He has hardly spoken about my uncle since his death."

Mr. Morrow nodded and gave me another smile, this one a bit warmer. "I assume it only had to do with the worries we all were sharing about the financial markets and what he might have known about that," he said, as if trying to make light of it. "What a terrible thing for him to be thinking of before he fell like that..."

I didn't quite know what to say in response, but it moved me to see Mr. Morrow concerned about my father.

"I am a bit worried that perhaps your father suspected your uncle's desire to take his own life and failed to convince him against it," Mr. Morrow said. "If true, it must be a sad load to carry. I wonder if that's why he does not wish to discuss it."

He shook his head abruptly. "I'm sorry to burden you with an old man's thoughts..." he said. "I imagine we have all been shaken enough over the events of the past few days. I do hope that you and your family will be able to have some peace."

"Thank you," I said uncertainly.

"Well, I had best be on my way," he said. "Keep an eye on your father for me, will you?"

"Of course," I said.

As he strode down the hall and out of sight, I let out a long, shaking breath I had been holding.

Was it possible what Mr. Morrow had suggested was true? That Father had somehow suspected Uncle Walter wanted to take his own life and had tried to change his mind?

Or was there something more sinister at work?

Whatever had truly happened, my father did not want to speak of it.

I tried to think back to the night of the dinner. I had paid little attention to who was where and when, apart from noticing the tension in the air from my father and some of his colleagues, Mr. Morrow and my uncle included. Jocelyn had made mention that there were people up speaking with Uncle Walter in his room. Was that before or after I had seen him near the dancers?

This still does not concern you, Sylvia, I scolded myself. *You wanted to be done with this, to step away.*

Then why did it seem as if I could not escape it? Why was it that every time I wanted out, I kept being dragged back in?

I shook my head, trying to clear the thoughts of what Mr. Morrow had said, and went to my father's door.

I knocked and he permitted entrance.

I found him sitting at his desk, writing a letter. It was a posture I had seen more often than not over the past days. I swallowed, not knowing where to start.

"I see you've returned from Walter's," he said, not looking up from the letter.

"Yes, Father," I said, clasping my hands in front of me to keep myself from fidgeting. "I apologize that I didn't come to you when Miles did, as Joan had something she wished to discuss with me."

"Did I hear you speaking with Frank out in the hall?" he asked, finally raising his eyes from the desk to stare hard at me.

My throat tightened and I clumsily cleared it. "Yes," I said. "He was asking after Joan, Mother, and I."

Father's eyes narrowed and I saw his lips tighten. "How little help he has been..." he mumbled, slowly lowering his head back to his letter. "He cannot seem to give me a straight answer about anything. I tell him not to try and spare my feelings, but he must be afraid of me chasing him away or some such nonsense."

My face flushed and I wanted nothing more than to excuse myself. He clearly was lost in his own mind, going through his thoughts. Had he already forgotten I was standing there in front of him?

"What did he ask you about Walter?" he asked, more to his paper than to me.

For a fraction of a second I considered not telling him but I knew that he could be testing me. If he had overheard what we spoke of, he would know if I lied.

"He wanted to know if I knew what you and Uncle Walter had discussed when you went up to his hotel room the night he – before he – " Why did I still struggle to say it out loud?

Snap went the pen against the desk. My father laid his hands on the desk before turning a sour expression up to me. "He did, did he?" he asked.

I resisted the urge to take a step backward. "Did you see Uncle Walter before he died?" I asked.

Father sighed, eyeing the desk. I wondered if he had even heard my question.

For a long, silent moment I stood there, uncertain whether I should move on or sit and wait.

"I did see your uncle," he said finally, folding his hands and turning to stare out the window that over-looked the back garden and the East River beyond. "I saw him and spoke with him...but I wasn't able to change his mind."

My stomach twisted. Did that mean Frank Morrow was right? Had Uncle Walter really killed himself? If that was true, then who wrote the letter that wasn't in his handwriting? And why had my uncle done it? What had he known?

"What – what were you unable to change his mind about?" I asked, feeling as unsteady as my voice sounded.

Father's brows knit together in the center of his forehead and he shifted his eyes to me. "About his marriage to Jocelyn Parker," he said, his tone holding a note of annoyance. "What did you think I was talking about?"

I took a step back, beneath the weight of his scrutinizing gaze. "I had no idea," I said. "Which is why I asked."

His suspicion wavered only a little and he looked back at his letter. "His marriage to her would have ruined his reputation and reflected poorly on the entire family," he said, picking up his pen again. "More importantly, that woman only wanted his wealth and would have drained him of every penny once they were married..." He paused. "But I suppose none of that matters now, does it?"

Why did Frank Morrow think Father was trying to convince Uncle Walter not to kill himself? I wondered when I was leaving his study a few minutes later. Was it possible Mr. Morrow and my father were talking about two different things, neither understanding what was on the other's mind?

I started down the hall and looked up as I heard approaching footsteps.

I found Miles making his way toward me with a tray laden with tea and a plate full of biscuits, likely sent up by our cook.

He smiled at me. "Hello, Miss Sylvia," he said, slowing as he drew nearer. "I hope the rest of your day is treating you well enough?"

"I suppose it is," I said, trying to smile.

His own expression faltered, giving way to a wrinkled brow. "You seem troubled," he said. "Did something happen with your father?"

"I – " I began, but stopped short. How was it he could so clearly read my emotions on my face? True, I was not precisely gifted at hiding them. Nonetheless, he seemed to have an understanding of me that not even my friends did, though I had only known him a few days. "It's nothing," I said, shaking my head, taking the silver key around my neck into my fingers again. "I suppose I am simply fatigued after the events of the past week."

He nodded. "I understand completely," he said. His gaze dropped to my fingers and to the key pressed tightly between them. "That necklace," he said with a small nod toward it. "I see you wearing it often. It must be rather special."

"It is," I said. "It once belonged to my grandmother."

It was nothing valuable but it unlocked a small, simple jewelry box that had long since been lost. The intricate carving of a vine wrapping around the key had been one of my grandmother's favorite keepsakes. Although it was not the only thing of hers that I had, it was just as much my favorite as it had been hers.

"A special memento, then," he said with a small smile. "I notice you take hold of it whenever you are worried. I suppose it is only natural that you would reach for something that once belonged to someone you trusted and took comfort in when troubled. It only makes sense."

I pulled the key forward to examine it. "I had never considered it that way."

He shifted the tray to his other hand. "Of course I do not wish to intrude, but if you are anxious about anything involving your uncle, I would be happy to help, if needed."

"I appreciate your offer," I said, consciously releasing the key in my hand. "Very much. If I am in need of anything, I will be sure to find you."

He didn't seem troubled that I had clearly not told him what had upset me, instead inclining his head and whistling as he made his way down to my father's study, disappearing inside with a bright "Here we are, sir, fresh tea and biscuits, just like my grandmother used to make."

I frowned, turning away.

There was something strange about this new butler of ours. Even Joan had noticed his astuteness and attention to detail. She knew nothing of his past or connections, his apparent understanding of dangerous situations and mysterious happenings... But for that matter, how much did I know about him, really?

As I walked up the stairs, pondering the question, it became clearer than ever that there was something secret...possibly even dark...about Miles and his past.

Whenever I asked how he came to know certain types of information, what experiences he'd had, he would brush the subject aside, ignore it, and steer the conversation away. It was clear he had no desire to speak of such things. But why? What was he afraid of? If any sort of wrong had been committed against him in the past, why keep quiet about it?

*Unless he had not been the victim of anything, but rather a perpetrator...*I thought as I closed my door behind myself, a cold, sinking feeling in the pit of my stomach. *What if he committed some sort of crime, perhaps back in England? And what if he fled to New York to escape it all?*

12

I became so consumed in my worries that afternoon that I had no appetite when the time for dinner came. I managed to push aside my questions about Miles, for the time being. It was not as if I had anything apart from my own feelings to justify such wild ideas. But the matter of Uncle Walter was not so easily dismissed. I found I could not stop thinking about the conversation my father had with Frank Morrow. Something about it simply did not sit well with me. It was the way Mr. Morrow had seemed to imply that my father had something to do with Uncle Walter's death.

I had known Frank Morrow for many years. Since I was a child, really. I had never heard him take any kind of defensive stance against my father, at least not about important matters. They had argued over business and investments throughout the years, but this was very different from that. This felt more personal. It seemed as if Mr. Morrow had grown suspicious over something, but I couldn't be sure of what or whether my father had done anything to deserve that suspicion.

This made me wonder about the connection Miles had suggested my uncle had with organized crime, and whether or not my father was caught up in any of that. From the way Mr. Morrow and my father had spoken of my uncle's *friends,* it was unlikely... But it did imply they each were aware such a connection existed for my uncle. Unless, of course, I had misunderstood the context of their remarks.

I sat on the cushioned seat of my windowsill, peering out onto the street below. The streetlights glowed brightly, like stationary fireflies. People raced by, attending to their normal lives...

Well, as normal as they can be with all that is going on in the world.

More than anything, I wished for life to go back to the way it was before that night at the hotel. I wanted my uncle back and I wanted my father to be himself again. But something else I wanted back was my own peace of mind. Now that my eyes had been opened to the family secrets swirling around me, it felt as if nothing could ever be the same again. My fleeting suspicions even of Miles were proof of my growing paranoia and distrust of everyone around me, something I had never felt before my uncle's death.

I despised the fact that I kept asking myself the same question, no matter how many times I tried to snuff it out; could my father have been involved in what happened to Uncle Walter? My first reaction every time was to say that no, of course he could not have. That thought was quickly followed by another, which said that I had to consider the possibility. I never would have believed my uncle could have criminal ties, and yet it seemed that he had. Did that mean everything I knew was not as it seemed? No. But did it mean that I needed to be open to the idea that my own father was not who I believed him to be? Yes. Yes, it did.

What if Mr. Morrow was right in suspecting something strange had happened that night in my uncle's room? My father had been acting rather bizarrely, almost ignoring the death of his brother as if it had never happened in the first place. I knew he cared about the financial state of our family, but his avoidance of the subject of Uncle Walter seemed out of character. What if he was trying to hide that he had – that he had somehow –

I pressed my fingers to my forehead, trying to stop the throbbing inside my skull.

*Something is not adding up...*I thought. My father was present with my family the night my uncle died. When I found them in the hotel lobby, they were all together.

There was no possible way that my father had been the shadowy figure I had glimpsed fleeing down that fire escape. It would be easy enough to check, as well, by asking Joan, or Mother, if he had ever left them –

The knock at my door sent me jumping to my feet, my heart pounding, my stomach in uncomfortable knots. "Who – who is it?" I asked. My throat hurt, and I knew the very expression on my face would make me appear guilty of something. I needed to calm myself.

"Miss Sylvia? My apologies, but I was sent to ask whether you will be coming down to dinner." I recognized Miles' voice through the door. "Is everything all right?"

"Yes, everything is fine," I answered without thinking. "But I'm not coming down."

"Would you care to have something brought up for you?" he asked.

"No," I said, a bit more firmly.

Silence met my words, and then my door swung inward.

"Pardon me, Miss Sylvia," he said from the doorway. "But are you certain nothing is wrong?"

He was as observant as usual, it seemed. No one else was troubled that I had been so distressed. My parents were lost in their own worlds, and my sister had managed to put aside whatever grief she might feel about Uncle Walter. But I had not, and somehow, Miles saw that.

"I do not mean to pry, but I have been worried about you all day," he said. "I knew something was the matter when I went in to see your father earlier and he was equally unsettled."

"He didn't tell you what happened?" I asked.

"I pointed out that his meeting with Mr. Morrow ended rather abruptly," he said. "He didn't say why, but I could sense it was not a pleasant departure."

"No..." I said. "I managed to overhear some of the conversation, and..." Once again, I didn't know how much to reveal. *But who else am I going to say it to? Who else would listen to me, or believe me?* "Mr. Morrow suspects my father of being involved with my uncle's death," I finally relented.

Miles' eyes grew gratifyingly wide; at least my own worries seemed justified now. "That is quite the accusation," he said. "I assume your father denied it?"

"Not outright," I said. "He simply dismissed Mr. Morrow, and – "

I stopped, my stomach twisting in knots.

Miles took a step into the room. "Are you all right?" he asked.

"The conversation they were having..." I said, looking up at Miles. "Something about it has not sat well with me."

"Why not?" he asked.

"They each seemed to think the other was talking about something they were not," I said, shaking my head. "What I mean is that my father mentioned he had not been able to convince my uncle of something, and never specified what it was to Mr. Morrow. When Mr. Morrow came out to speak with me, he said he thought my father had not been able to convince my uncle against taking his own life, but my father told me he had not been able to change my uncle's mind about marrying Jocelyn Parker."

Miles' mouth opened slightly, and understanding flickered behind his eyes. "That is interesting," he said, dropping his voice. "It leads one to wonder, did either of them know about that letter on your uncle's desk?"

I hurried to my desk, pulling the drawer out and taking the letter from within. I quickly read through it again. "Reading this now, I am more certain than ever that this is not my uncle's letter. It doesn't even sound like a letter he would write. It isn't his tone."

"And you said it wasn't his handwriting," Miles said. "And your father...did he even mention your uncle committing suicide in his discussion with Mr. Morrow?"

"No," I said. "That's what has been troubling me, though I hadn't realized it. Apart from you and I, I haven't heard anyone else suggest that could have been the case."

"What, then, was the reason for him saying that to you?" Miles asked. "Perhaps to plant the idea in your mind?"

A cold shiver raced through me. "But why?" I asked. "Why would he – " I gasped, grabbing Miles' arm to steady myself. I stared at him. "Miles, what if it wasn't my father at all, but Frank Morrow?"

Miles searched my face, his own thoughtful. "Go on," he said.

Memories of the past week, containing Mr. Morrow, burst through the fog in my thoughts like brilliant sunbeams, all lining up one next to the other. "Frank Morrow has been a financial advisor to both my father and my uncle for a number of years, their friend even longer," I said. "A point he deemed important enough to mention when speaking with my father, as if to remind him."

Miles nodded. "That would make sense."

"My father and my uncle have always trusted Mr. Morrow, and Mr. Morrow even mentioned that he may not have always seen eye to eye with them, but he always considered them friends. How did I not consider him as a possible suspect? He was there that night at the hotel. He surely would have been one of the ones invited up to see my uncle's room, would have known where he was staying," I said.

My heart quickened, as I looked at Miles.

"They all shared the same associations...and Mr. Morrow would have known of my uncle's criminal connections, just as my father did," I said. It startled me just how crystal clear this all suddenly was. "But my father said something that still confuses me..."

"What was that?" Miles asked.

"Mr. Morrow asked my father what he and my uncle had spoken about when it was just the two of them. My father said he wondered when Mr. Morrow would turn the blame on to him," I said.

Miles frowned, but didn't turn away. "It is typical for a criminal to deflect blame for their actions on to someone else."

I wrapped my arms around myself, suddenly chilled all the way through.

"How confident are you that it might have been him?" Miles asked. "This is the first time we have discussed the possibility."

"I don't know," I said, shrugging. "Now I am not so sure."

"What was Mr. Morrow's relationship with your uncle?" Miles asked. "Same as with your father?"

I nodded. "Yes. The three of them were often together, but why would he want my uncle dead?"

"Have you an example of his handwriting to compare to the suicide note?" Miles asked.

I shook my head. "And I don't know if my father would either," I said. "Mr. Morrow has always been the sort to deliver messages in person or over the telephone."

Miles nodded. "That certainly makes things harder on us."

"Of everyone that it could have been…" I muttered, shaking my head.

"You said he and your uncle were friends," Miles said. "How close?"

I rubbed my arms. "I do not know," I said. "They may not have been as friendly as Mr. Morrow and my father were." I swallowed hard. "Something happened that night, and it seems that Mr. Morrow has a far darker view of the whole affair than my father. Father wanted to change Uncle Walter's mind about marrying Jocelyn. Mr. Morrow seemed suspicious, overly so, and then the way he planted that idea in my head that my father might have had something to do with the suicide…"

"If he wrote the note – " Miles said.

" – Then he would have of course known what was written on it!" I said.

"You are exactly right," Miles said. "That very well might have been a slip on his part. He has no idea that you are looking into your uncle's death, right?"

"I highly doubt it," I said. "The only other person who knows is Joan, and she only learned that a few hours ago."

"Then we have a suspect," Miles said.

"But what do we do?" I asked.

"We have to find a way to prove it was him," Miles said.

"How? Do we go and ask him questions?" I asked. "I couldn't do that. He would see through me in an instant."

"Not if he doesn't suspect it has anything to do with your uncle..." Miles said, his gaze suddenly vacant, sweeping the floor as he thought hard. "If you could distract him for long enough, I could slip in and look around for some sort of evidence."

"Such as what?" I asked. "I wouldn't know where to begin."

"Anything, really," he said with a shrug. "You would be amazed what could tie someone to a crime."

"But how would you know it when you saw it?" I asked.

"Perhaps I could find a sample of his handwriting?" he asked.

"I already told you, he doesn't send letters," I said. "He takes his messages to people in person."

"Everyone jots down an occasional note, even if it's only a reminder for themselves. Regardless, I could see what I could find," he said. "What do you say? Would you like my help?"

I hesitated. "I told myself I was done with this whole thing..." I said.

Miles regarded me patiently. "If that is your wish, we

need not do anything." His green eyes flashed. "However, you have acquired more knowledge than perhaps anyone else about all this. It could be of great value."

I hesitated. "I am not cut out for this," I said. "I wouldn't know what to do if we did find out he was the murderer."

"We would take the information to the proper authorities and allow them to handle it from there," Miles said. "We could go right now but having more proof would spur them on faster. They may not take the case if we have only suspicion, no matter how solid it is."

I glanced out the window. The sun had dipped below the buildings along the western side of the city, casting long shadows over the road, blanketing the motorcars as they drove through Sutton Place. "What will I say to him?" I asked. "I have never tried to stall for time. I'm not the best liar."

"You don't need to be," Miles said, sweeping out through the door. "You just need to be good at making conversation with an old family friend."

Before I realized it, I had followed Miles down the stairs and out to the car, where we started off.

IT WASN'T until we were half a mile from Frank Morrow's house that I began to regret my decision. The only solace I had was that I would not be the one snooping around, and that my responsibility would likely be far easier and far less sneaky.

"You need not worry," Miles said, parking the car along the side of the street. He waited until another car blazed by, its horn blaring. "I will be able to get in and out without being seen."

I wanted to question how, exactly, he had so much confidence in such things, but I held my tongue. It occurred to me to wonder just why Miles was so willing to help me with all this in the first place. Every time I tried to let go of my uncle's death, Miles was insistent that we had to get to the truth, together.

I banished the thought as quickly as it flickered through my mind, however. I didn't want to consider its implications. I had liked Miles from the moment I met him and, despite all his inexplicable little inconsistencies, I still did.

I re-focused my mind on Frank Morrow and the plan before me.

It shouldn't have surprised me when Mr. Morrow's butler warmly welcomed me into his home, Miles lingering out on the steps, unnoticed as most chauffeurs usually were, and Mr. Morrow sent for. I gave Miles a wary look as the door closed between us, and all I received was a firm, small nod.

He really is going to do this, isn't he? How and when, I

had no idea...but I needed to do what I could to protect him.

When Frank Morrow learned of my arrival, he hurried down to greet me. He paused at the top of the stunning stairwell, which swept around in a half circle down to the floor below, wide and luxurious. It was perhaps my favorite characteristic of his whole house, and I could remember Joan and me peering through the banisters at the top, staring down into the foyer while Mother and Father talked to Mr. Morrow and his late wife, Lillian.

"What a pleasant surprise," he said, beaming at me as he came down the magnificent staircase. "I hope your father has not sent you on some errand for him?"

"You are most observant," I said, trying my best to appear as innocent as possible. "It isn't anything much, just a book or two."

Mr. Morrow's eyes darted to my hands, where two books I had taken randomly from Father's office were tightly held. He nodded. "Ah, yes. He did mention sending something...but that was some weeks ago... No matter." He grinned. "Might I offer you hot tea or coffee? It seems Winter is encroaching upon us, and I must admit I am simply not ready for it this year."

"Nor am I," I said, pleased that I could be so very honest, at least with that statement.

"Come along, then," he said. "I am sure your father will forgive me for taking a little of your time."

"That would be wonderful, thank you," I said, relieved that I would not have to make up some excuse, such as asking for tea myself, in order to buy Miles time. I turned to look, and I could still see Miles out on the front steps through the window. He met my gaze and smiled.

*I hope this works...*I thought as I followed Mr. Morrow into the drawing room off the front entry hall.

Mr. Morrow had furnished his drawing room much like my family had, with comfortable seating for quite a few guests, purposely arranged for entertaining and parties. I imagined it had not housed many of those in the past few days, as hardly anyone else had, but I noticed the chess board near the fireplace had been set and ready, the buffet along the back wall stocked with fresh teacups all lined in a neat row, and chairs arranged in circles prepared for conversation.

"I apologize for the mess," he said, gesturing to a stack of linens near the door. "As I know your father has done, I have had to prepare for the possibility of selling some of my belongings." He didn't finish his thought, but I knew it was just in case things on Wall Street did not turn around...as they had not yet seemed to.

"It's no trouble," I said. I set the books down on one of the nearby tables, and took the seat beside it.

Mr. Morrow strode to the window, peering out into the street. "It's been quite a week, hasn't it?" he asked.

"I spoke with my girls earlier today. Both seem to be doing well, as are their husbands. They think they will be able to weather all this."

"That is good to hear," I said. His daughters were older than Joan and I, but I had always liked them. "I heard that Mr. Henry is considering selling his home."

Mr. Morrow turned at that, his eyes widening. "Really?" he asked. "Your father didn't mention that when I saw him."

"Yes, well...perhaps I should not have said anything either," I said, my face flushing.

My heart thumped uncomfortably in my chest, and I wondered where in the world Miles must be. I didn't think he was likely still lingering out on the front steps, but did that mean he was inside, looking around already? What had he found? Would he signal to me somehow? Or should I simply guess when it would be safe to leave?

"It's of no matter," Mr. Morrow said with a warm smile. "I would have learned soon enough. That's too bad, really. He isn't the first I have heard making such decisions. I believe it is all slightly rash. People are reacting far too emotionally and will regret their decisions in coming weeks."

I nodded, uncertain how to continue. I was worse at all this than I had thought I would be.

"So..." he said, turning to me as his butler strode into the room, carrying a silver tray with a carafe and two cups on it. "Your father told me there is a new young man in your life."

"Really?" I asked. "I am not aware of any such person." I couldn't think who he meant.

"Well, perhaps now I am the one who has spoken too soon," he said. "I believe there is someone he is hoping to introduce you to. Quite a wealthy fellow, from what I hear. Your father hopes you will take a fancy to one another. A Mr. Phillips, I believe? His father owns part of a coal factory down in Pennsylvania. He would be a catch, even in these...uncertain times."

I did not have time or the energy to consider a stranger my father had told me nothing about.

Mr. Morrow thanked his butler, who excused himself from the room.

"Sugar in your coffee?" he asked.

I nodded warily.

"Milk?"

"Yes, please," I said.

"Oh, and I was pleased to hear that your father finally hired a new butler," he said as he poured the steaming coffee into the pair of mugs.

I nearly swallowed my tongue. Of *all* the things he could have mentioned – "Oh, ye – yes," I stuttered. "He just started."

"Excellent," Mr. Morrow said. "I hope he is as loyal to your family as old Theodore was."

"Miles has been more than satisfactory thus far," I said. "Very attentive. And intuitive."

"Is that so?" Mr. Morrow asked.

"He is also our chauffeur," I said. I spat out the words so quickly that I only realized after I had spoken that in my desperation to find something to talk about, I might have been talking *too* much about him. "He drove me here today, in fact. He is likely around, if you wish to meet him."

Mr. Morrow, whose back was turned to me, slowly set the carafe down onto the tray. "He's around, you say?" he asked. He turned to me, a curious glint in his eye. "In the car, you mean, waiting for you?"

"Y – Yes," I said, unable to meet his gaze. I brushed some stray hair behind my ear, my hand inadvertently shaking. "I believe so, at least. Why would he be anywhere else?"

I was making this worse by the second.

"I am impressed that your new butler would be the one to drive you all the way out here..." Mr. Morrow said, walking over to hand me my coffee. "Just to deliver some books."

I said nothing, only taking the cup from his outstretched hand.

"What did you say he did before he came to work for your father?" he asked.

"I – " I said, trying to make my brain work faster than his suddenly seemed to be. "I didn't say."

"Well, who did he work for?" Mr. Morrow asked.

"I – " I said. "I am not sure. He has not shared that information with me."

Mr. Morrow's fingers drummed against the side of his cup. Had my awkward behavior made him suspicious?

"You wouldn't mind if I went to find this new butler of yours and introduced myself, would you?" he asked, setting his cup down and already halfway to the door before all the words had left his mouth.

"Wait!" I said, leaping to my feet.

Mr. Morrow didn't listen, striding out into the foyer.

My head swam as I started after him, fearing seeping through every vein in my body, stretching all the way to the tips of my fingers. Why had I been so foolish? Why hadn't I steered the conversation away like I should have?

"Don't worry, Sylvia," Mr. Morrow said as I reached him out in the foyer, already halfway up the stairs. "I don't expect you to understand the real reason why your father sent you all the way out here."

"What do you mean?" I asked, hurrying up after him.

"He sent you here to try and find information," he said, his eyes blazing. "And is using that new butler of yours to do it."

13

Icy, prickling fear filled my chest as it struck me just how perceptive Mr. Morrow was... and how quickly he had deduced the exact reason why I was there. He might have been wrong that it had been my father who had sent me, but he was not at all wrong about why Miles was here.

"Mr. Morrow – " I said as I hurried up the stairs after him, unable to think quickly enough to know what I should say to stop what he was doing. "Mr. Morrow, please – why would our chauffeur come up here? There would be no reason."

"That's precisely my question," he said. "Why would he want to come up here?"

"I assure you, he isn't here," I said. "What I think is happening is that we have all had some very stressful days this week and that is causing us to jump to conclusions."

"Perhaps you are right," he said, but pushed open the first door to his left all the same.

"I imagine he is out by the car right now," I said. "Likely reading a book while he waits for me."

Mr. Morrow stopped then, and turned around. "Blake!" he called down the stairs. "Go out to Mr. Shipman's car and find the chauffeur," he said.

"Right away, sir," said the butler from downstairs.

My insides rolled over. I knew when he went out there, he wouldn't find Miles.

"What did you say his name was?" Mr. Morrow asked, giving me a tight, brief smile over his shoulder. "Murphy, I believe?"

"Miles," I said automatically, before realizing I should not have answered that question.

"Miles!" Mr. Morrow called, strolling down the hall. The jovial tone in his voice set my nerves on edge, like the feeling I had when grinding my teeth. "Oh, Miles, are you up here? Uninvited, in my home?"

I slowed, watching him walk to the doors up and down the hall, pushing them open, humming an offkey tune under his breath.

My heart thundered at each door, waiting for him to spring upon Miles, catching him rifling through a drawer, finding him in the midst of his search. Each empty room only increased the chances.

I followed him to even the third floor...but he didn't find him.

Where had he gone?

Mr. Morrow, likewise, seemed even more suspicious.

I did my best to smile at him from the stairwell. "See?" I told him. "He wouldn't have come all the way up here. Just as I said."

Mr. Morrow searched my face, wearing an expression of anger I had never seen directed at me before. "...Very well," he said, and strode past me toward the stairs.

He had just reached the second story landing, about to head down to the foyer, when Miles appeared, striding up the stairs. "Mr. Morrow, sir?" he asked. He inclined his head. "My apologies. I have been told you were looking for me."

Blake, Mr. Morrow's butler, hurried up the stairs after Miles. "Sir – sir!" he said, breathing heavily. He took hold of the railing, standing on the second stair from the top, leaning over as he drew in deep breaths. "Mr. Morrow, I went out to the car as you asked, and this man was nowhere near it. I couldn't find him anywhere!"

Mr. Morrow stood a bit straighter, looking down at Miles, folding his arms.

"Of course I wasn't by the car," Miles said smoothly. "I was in the back seat of the car, lying across the back, trying to repair a tear in the carpet." He looked at Mr. Morrow with a steady, patient gaze that made me think he might actually be telling the truth. "You are welcome to go and inspect my work, if you wish."

Mr. Morrow's hardened expression didn't change. "Turn out your pockets," he said, his gaze sweeping up the length of Miles' coat.

Miles didn't respond immediately, staring in challenge up at Mr. Morrow.

I heard a clink of metal...and turned to see Mr. Morrow pull a gun from the inside pocket of his own coat. In one smooth movement, he pointed it straight at Miles who stood at the top of the stairs.

MY KNEES WENT weak and I had to take hold of the banister beside me to stop from falling over.

No one said anything. No one moved. I couldn't hear anything apart from my pulse thundering inside my skull.

Miles slowly raised his hands up on either side of himself. "I will turn out my pockets...if you promise not to shoot when I move."

Mr. Morrow's jaw clenched, and he nodded, his finger inching toward the trigger.

Miles reached slowly into his pocket and withdrew a small red book.

"That's the book we found at my uncle's," I said, recognizing it. I had forgotten Miles had kept it.

Miles nodded. "I've tucked a letter inside for safe keeping. Something written in Mr. Morrow's hand."

Evidently I had been wrong in saying Mr. Morrow never wrote anything down. Miles must have snatched a letter or note he'd found somewhere in this house.

"Where did you get any letter of mine?" Mr. Morrow asked. "You did sneak around! You did go into my study!"

His hand swung around, shifting the barrel of the gun to point at me.

"And you!" he spat. "What do you have to do with this? How did you get caught up in snooping through my things?"

My heart raced but I still felt the need to say what was on my mind. "I never wanted to believe my father's worries about you over the past few years..." I murmured. "I always thought he was growing needlessly paranoid. It's clear to me now *why* he was so concerned. Innocent people do not pull out a gun so easily. I see now there is more to you than I realized."

Mr. Morrow said nothing, his jaw working, his face suddenly revealing a surprising sadness.

"My uncle had connections with powerful criminals here in town," I said. "I had no idea until recently. *That* is what my father was so troubled over...and then he must have learned that you, too, had the same connections. It would explain everything, wouldn't it? His distrust, it seems, was well founded."

Mr. Morrow swallowed, glancing over at Miles, a wild and panicked look coming into his eyes.

"You all have the same ties," I said. "At least, that is what my father thought. He trusted you and my uncle. But all the while you both were involving yourselves with dangerous people and schemes. Tell me, Mr. Morrow, was it worth it?"

My fear had subsided as my anger grew. "This is what got my uncle killed, wasn't it?" I demanded. "And you knew something about it. That's why you went in to see my father, to try and find some way to pin it on him. You must have thought that if you could get him to slip, get *me* to slip, that one of us would tell you *something* you could use to make the death seem like Father's fault. But you made a mistake, Mr. Morrow, when coming out to speak with me in the hall as you did this afternoon." I swallowed, the passion welling up in my throat, making it tight. "I deserve to know what you had to do with my uncle's death! I deserve to know if you were the one to leave that note in his room, claiming he was taking his own life!"

"It was all his fault!" Mr. Morrow bellowed, startling me with his shift in temper. Whatever regret I had detected in his face earlier was gone now. His voice swallowed up my own as it bounced around the foyer, down the stairs, echoing off the walls and floors. "He was the one who managed to get me all tied up in it. He convinced me to take a deal that looked ominous, assuring me all the while there was nothing to worry about, that all the investments were clean and sound. He *lied to me!* Walter became a different man once he fell in with his new *associates*. All he could think about was money! And he was ready to betray or entangle anyone to get it, even me!"

I could only stare at him, dumbfounded by the words that spilled out of his mouth.

"You may have thought you knew your uncle, but you knew nothing!" Mr. Morrow spat. "He became hungry for power, for extravagant wealth... His new *friends* promised to grow his fortune with no worries. All he had to do was pay the horrendous prices they asked of him, such as brokering a crooked deal, arranging an invitation to an exclusive event, or perhaps the worst one...providing the name and address of a particular person who ended up dead the following day."

My mouth went dry. Uncle Walter...was he really talking about *my* uncle?

"He got me all caught up in their trap, tied me up so tight I knew I could never escape it. They would never let me out of their organization, even if I tried," he said.

I thought back to when Miles had essentially said the same thing about my uncle, that if he was involved with such criminals they almost certainly had something to do with his death. I wondered wildly how in the world he had known that. Was *he* involved in all this, too?

"There is no excuse great enough to explain why you did what you did," Miles said, breaking my attention and my train of thought.

I looked around at him, my heart pounding.

"I know you are the one who killed Walter Shipman..." Miles went on, his brow set, his green eyes blazing. "...And I have the proof."

14

"What proof do you have?" Mr. Morrow asked. It struck me that he didn't deny it outright.

Miles, to my surprise, let out a bark of a laugh, which sounded bizarre and out of place coming from him. "Why would I be fool enough to share that?" he asked.

Mr. Morrow's grip on the gun tightened and he straightened his slackening arm, setting the barrel on Miles once more. "Blake, go down and lock the door," he told his butler in a low voice. "These two are not leaving here."

Blake, however, who had not left his place on the stairs just behind Miles, seemed frozen in place.

Mr. Morrow's gaze snapped over to the man, his

face darkening. "I said go and lock the door!" he demanded.

Blake stared at Mr. Morrow with abject horror, his mouth slightly open.

*He must be as shocked by all this as I am...*I thought bitterly.

"This all makes a great deal of sense, really," Miles said as Mr. Morrow ran his fingers through his hair. "First, the planted note in Walter Shipman's room. It was not written in his hand. A hasty, sloppy move, but I suppose you had little time to really flesh out a plan, did you?" He reached into the front of the book, extracting the letter he had mentioned. "All we would need to do is compare this letter, penned in your own hand, to the note found in his hotel room. I imagine we would find a perfect match, wouldn't we?"

I hardly dared to breathe, watching both Mr. Morrow's face as well as Miles'. A battle of wills was taking place and I wondered who was going to blink first.

"Second, you have already confessed before us all to having been dragged into illegal activities, and although you claim it was against your will, I am certain the proper authorities will be very interested in your connections."

Mr. Morrow opened his mouth to speak, but Miles jumped to it first.

"And lastly..." Miles said. "Though I suppose I

cannot reason what happened precisely, something occurred that you didn't want any part of. It is clear you despised Walter Shipman for involving you in crooked deals, yes? So what happened that night he died? That night when you pushed him?"

Mr. Morrow said nothing for a long, hard minute. My heartbeats counted the seconds as they passed, until he spoke. "He asked the unthinkable of me..." he said. "He had learned the stock market would take a drastic fall come morning. He said some of his insider friends claimed they had seen the numbers, and he knew that with all his investments, he would be done for."

"What did he ask of you?" Miles asked.

"He told me if I didn't want to lose everything, not only my money, but his money, Cecil's money, all the money of those I advised professionally... I had to go along with some plan he had devised, or his *friends* had devised, to capitalize on the market fall. I refused, told him he had lost his mind – but that didn't matter. He wouldn't listen."

"He put you in an impossible situation," Miles said.

"But instead of talking it through with him..." I breathed. "You just...pushed him over the side? You killed him because..." I could hardly form the words. "Because why?"

"He was going to send those criminals after me for refusing to cooperate, I know he was," he said. "Walter wouldn't hear reason. I told him I would be able to help navigate through any downturn that might occur, that he wouldn't need to keep relying on those people for help when they clearly were not providing him with any." He grimaced, absently lowering the gun. "He was far too concerned with his own money than the consequences of being tied up with dangerous people. He simply didn't care about the risks. In our argument, he kept goading me, telling me what a fool I was – and before I realized what had happened...he was already falling."

Silence filled the room, stilling every breath. He had admitted to it. He had killed my uncle...and now...

He blinked, staring around at all three of us.

"I – " he said, his face blotchy and red all of a sudden. He rubbed his face, sweat streaking his temples. "I – I didn't – That is I mean I – "

"It will be better for you if you cooperate now," Miles said, chancing a step forward.

Mr. Morrow didn't seem to notice, his wide eyes vacant and distant.

"I...I cannot be caught," he said. "If those gangsters find out that I – that I had any connection to his death..." His face paled. "They will kill me."

He looked around, making eye contact with each of us in turn.

He raised the gun for a third time, this time pointing it right at me. A fat tear splashed out onto his face, trailing down his cheek. "I'm sorry..." he murmured.

I knew what was about to happen. There was nothing I could do but close my eyes.

Something hard struck me in the side, at the same moment that fingers coiled around my wrist, shoving me away from the side of the railing. My eyes flew open just as I slammed into the floor behind a marble statue along the back wall, away from the stairs. Nearby, another statue lay on the floor. Miles must have shoved it over to knock me aside and distract Mr. Morrow.

I scrambled up onto my elbows just in time to see Miles reach Mr. Morrow, who stood stunned by his quick movements. He managed to grab the gun before Mr. Morrow could pull the trigger. It clattered to the floor, sliding all the way to the edge of the stairs, teetering on the lip of a step.

I looked around. There had to be something I could find to help Miles, to protect us –

Mr. Morrow grabbed Miles by the back of his shirt, whipping him around. Even if he didn't have a weapon any longer, it was clear that he had no intention of letting us leave.

He forced Miles down to his knees, but Miles seemed prepared, kicking his legs out in a sweeping motion, knocking Mr. Morrow's legs out from underneath him.

I snatched a bronze vase off the long table beside me, and held it up to throw in our enemy's direction. If I could just catch him off guard, I might be able buy Miles enough time to get away, to try and run –

But then what? What could we possibly do to get out of this horrible situation?

"They can never know!" Mr. Morrow cried, rolling to his side, already starting to get up. "They just can't!"

The fear in his voice stayed my hand, and my breath caught in my chest.

I couldn't throw it. I couldn't harm Mr. Morrow, my father's old friend, a man who had chased me around the garden as a child, as I laughed and played with him and his own daughter, a man who had given me so much of his time and attention –

He lifted his foot into the air and kicked Miles in the side of the head. Miles fell to the ground with a sickening thud, and didn't rise.

Mr. Morrow stood over him, breathing heavily, his expression wild.

He wasn't the man I had known. He had changed... and he had killed my uncle.

I wound up, and with as much strength as I could muster, threw the heavy vase toward him.

It struck him in the shoulder, sending him off balance. He flailed his arms like a windmill, but he fell backward. He struck the banister, grasping for the handrail, but he had built up too much momentum and fell backward over the side of the railing.

He let out a terrible cry before he struck the floor below with a *smash* that sent chills up my spine.

"Miss Sylvia – "

I turned to see Miles rushing toward me.

"Are you all right?" he asked.

"I'm fine," I said, though my voice cracked. "Mr. Morrow, is he – "

Blake stared over the side of the railing, his face pale.

"You stay up here, Miss Sylvia..." Miles said. "I will go and see what happened."

I nodded numbly, and he and Blake made their way down the stairs.

With shaky knees, I hobbled over to the railing. I wanted to see if he – if he –

I caught a glimpse of his legs...one of which lay splayed out at an odd angle.

I turned away, unable to look any more. It was a scene too reminiscent of that other death, the one that had started all this.

15

"I appreciate your father's willingness to allow me to move my quarters," Miles said as he carried a box through a door at the end of the western hall of the house.

I threw open the drapes to allow daylight into the space. "Well, I don't believe we could have expected you to remain in a room where a brick was thrown through the window," I said. "Not when it is becoming so cold so quickly."

"It's astonishing just how frigid this part of the world becomes," Miles said, setting the box down on the writing desk along the wall. He had yet to move his bed or most of his other belongings. "It almost makes me miss London. Almost."

"You'd best prepare yourself for much colder

nights," Mrs. Riley said, striding into the room with a stack of fresh linens in her arms. "It only becomes more difficult from here."

"I appreciate the words of encouragement, Mrs. Riley," Miles said with a small laugh. "And thank you for your assistance."

Mrs. Riley gave a dismissive wave as she exited the room as quickly as she had entered it.

"I think she's a little irritated at having to make up another new room for me so soon after I've moved in," Miles confided.

"Did anyone ever learn *why* there was a brick thrown through your window?" The question came from Joan, who poked her head in to see what all the commotion was about.

"Just some drunk passerby, it seems," I said with a sigh. "Rather unhappy about the state of his life, or so the police told Father."

Joan shook her head. "We could all do with this nonsense fixing itself, couldn't we?"

"Miss Joan, your mother is looking for you," Mrs. Riley said, striding past the open door in the opposite direction.

Joan gave me a pointed look. "Oh, wonderful. I imagine she has another riveting story to share. Sylvia, won't you come with me?"

"I will be there shortly," I said. "I just need to move some of my belongings out of here."

She headed out, leaving Miles and I to continue our work.

"So, how are you holding up?" Miles asked.

I hesitated just before the wardrobe, which held a number of dresses that had been handed down to me by my cousins. The spare room Miles was being given had previously been used for the storage of miscellaneous household items, including some old clothing of mine and Joan's.

"I'm well, thank you for asking," I said, pulling the doors open and beginning to drape the dresses over my arm.

"That's not what I meant," he said.

I turned to find him staring intently at me.

I swallowed hard. I knew what he meant. "I'm as well as one can be under the circumstances, I suppose," I said. "I keep having dreams, of course."

"Nightmares?" he asked.

I turned away, pulling more dresses from the wardrobe. "Yes."

In my mind's eye, I again imagined Frank Morrow's lifeless body lying on the floor, looking so like my Uncle Walter's corpse had also looked that night in the hotel lobby.

The aftermath of the struggle in Mr. Morrow's house was already a blur in my memory. The butler, Blake, had immediately telephoned the police to inform them of events, and then Miles had telephoned my father. Father had arrived with our family attorney in tow, and the attorney ensured my questioning from the police was minimal. Miles and I were allowed to leave quickly, with the unfortunate Mr. Blake being left behind to give a longer statement. Because he lived in the same house as the deceased, the police seemed more interested in what goings on the servant had witnessed than in the final confrontation Miles and I had shared with Frank Morrow. I had the sense they were quite excited about Mr. Morrow's criminal connections and where an investigation of those might lead...

I shook the thoughts from my mind and tried to focus on the present. All of that was resolved now. Father would deal with any lingering issues, should the police need more information.

"Those bad dreams will go away," Miles was saying. "I wish I could tell you when, but it may not be for some time."

I nodded. "That is what I assumed."

"I heard your father say the police have matched the handwriting from the note and the letter," Miles said. "They confirmed what happened to your uncle."

"I know," I said. "Father and my Uncle Jack are working together to finally arrange a funeral for Uncle Walter."

"That is right and good," Miles said.

I was silent.

"I will return shortly," he said. "Take all the time you need gathering your things."

I nodded.

Miles strode from the room, leaving me with my thoughts.

I glanced briefly over at one of the boxes he had brought into the room earlier, stacked neatly beside others.

My heart skipped a few beats as I noticed the corner of a small, red book peeking out.

It couldn't be –

Without thinking, I bent down and snatched the book from the box. My heart pounded as I stared down at it, willing it not to be what it looked like.

An elegant script along the spine announced that it was a title on gardening.

It was not the book from Uncle Walter's house. Miles had told me he turned that over to my father, who had passed it on to the authorities. Evidently, he had not lied about that.

I sighed, relief washing over me.

My face flushed as I realized that I had picked something out of one of Miles' boxes without his permission. I wasted no time trying to put the book back, only to catch it on the corner of the box, which sent it flying across the floor.

When the book struck the floor, the front cover opened and a yellowed piece of paper fell out, fluttering through the air.

I hurried over, grabbing the book and the scrap of loose paper. I should put everything back quickly, before Miles returned to find me seemingly snooping through his things.

I set the paper down inside the front cover, and realized it was a clipping from a newspaper. The name of the paper had been cut off, but I could still read *NDON TIMES.*

It must be from his time in London, I thought.

The article was torn in half, only the first paragraphs still intact. It read: *A wealthy young socialite was found in Hyde Park early Tuesday morning, dead. The matter is still under investigation, but authorities have received an anonymous tip indicating the victim was killed by none other than her husband.*

A chill ran down my spine as I glanced at the picture beneath the article. It showed a beautiful young woman...standing beside a man who was most certainly Miles.

In that instant, all of the air suddenly seemed to be sucked from the room. My mind spun dizzily, trying to make sense of what I was seeing. I had thought I was done with dark secrets and dangerous people.

Now it seemed I had simply stepped out of one mystery and into another...

Continue the mysterious adventures of Sylvia Shipman in "Murder With Means: A Sylvia Shipman Murder Mystery Book 2."

ABOUT THE AUTHOR

Blythe Baker is the lead writer behind several popular historical and paranormal mystery series. When Blythe isn't buried under clues, suspects, and motives, she's acting as chauffeur to her children and head groomer to her household of beloved pets. She enjoys walking her dogs, lounging in her backyard hammock, and fiddling with graphic design. She also likes binge-watching mystery shows on TV. To learn more about Blythe, visit her website and sign up for her newsletter at www.blythebaker.com

Printed in Great Britain
by Amazon

18821784R00123